Magassus Mountain

By

Arlene Johnston

First edition

Pine Lake Books
West Guilford, ON

Library and Archives Canada Cataloguing in Publication

Johnston, Arlene, 1951-
    Magassus Mountain / by Arlene Johnston. -- 1st ed.

Issued also in electronic format.
ISBN 978-1-926898-26-1

    I. Title.

PS8619.O4845M34 2012   jC813'.6   C2012-900923-7

Library and Archives Canada Cataloguing in Publication

Johnston, Arlene, 1951-
    Magassus Mountain [electronic resource] / by Arlene Johnston. -- 1st ed.

Electronic monograph.
Issued also in print format.
ISBN 978-1-926898-27-8

    I. Title.

PS8619.O4845M34 2012   jC813'.6   C2012-900924-5

West Guilford
www.pinelakebooks.ca

Book One

DEMPSTER

Dempster is more determined than ever to live alone on the Magassus Mountain now that his family has deserted him. Anger and bitterness are his driving force as he rebels against the 'Law of Nature'.

Chapter 1: Beth

ARMAND COULD NOT believe his good fortune of finding a mate and a home in the same week. *Crows are not usually this lucky* he thought smugly circling back toward the mountain cliff for one last gander. *My adversaries will be so envious it may cause a riot,* he chuckled, flying back to collect his mate.

Armand had always enjoyed the challenge. He was headstrong and fearless. This coupled with his superior intelligence and size made him triumphantly a leader of the pack.

As he flew back into the valley, the field behind Metcalf's barn was alive with crows pecking the ground for buried grains in the abandoned cornfield. Perching on the rusty weather vane located in the center of the roof on the old faded grey barn he had a bird's eye view of all the activities below. His eyes scanned the snow dotted field. They seemed to know exactly where to look in a field occupied by close to 100 crows. *There she is* he thought, breathing deeply, expanding his chest in self-assured pride.

Beth was the most beautiful crow Armand had ever laid his coal black eyes on. He remembered their courtship dance, passed on from generation to generation and the competition with other males also in pursuit of his chosen. Beth's reluctance as she pretended to be completely unaware of her suitors. How she would not look directly at Armand and turned her head away. He loved the challenge for he knew it was just a matter of time before he would win her over. He chuckled to himself as he thought about the final scenario. Beth had flown a short distance with Armand and the last rival still in pursuit.

When two males court the same female and she shows no definite preference, a contest begins. Armand and his rival flew straight up clashing in mid-air, each trying to rise above the other, battering with wings and bills. So intense was the fighting that they fell to the ground rolling about; the weaker crow finally submitted and flew away. *Yes, I won the fight,* Armand thought, perched above eyeing his future in the late morning sun.

He flew down to Beth and proceeded to tell her about their new home on Magassus Mountain.

"On a mountain? I like it here near this field with the others close by," Beth said hesitantly.

Crows usually favour woodlands and farmlands but have been known to break protocol and nest on mountains.

"The mountain is only a few days journey away." Armand looked toward the trees surrounding the cornfield. "All the trees in this area are filling up quickly. I believe we should have our own distinct territory to establish ourselves and raise our family," Armand coaxed.

It didn't take much more persuading to sway Beth, for Armand was her mate and she was very proud of him. She had fallen head over claws for him. She was sure Armand knew what he was doing removing them from the flock. With a wink and a nudge from Armand, the pair flew off.

Magassus Mountain stood alone rising up to meet the clear spring day. Waves of green drawn up the sides indicated its plush vegetation, more than ample in which to build a new home. Their flight went without incident. Beth's reluctance soon dissolved into joy as she strutted around the foreign territory she would now call home. The area of mountain Armand had chosen was on the leeward side, not too far up from the valley below, where several streams flowed into a small lake. When days grew longer in spring or shorter in the fall, migrating crows will pass through the valley enabling Armand, Beth, and their offspring to join the migrating flocks.

They constructed their nest under a large grassy over-hang that would provide ample protection from the elements, while seconding as a lookout post for predators. Though the area was quite rocky, tufts of grass sprouted throughout and moss grew plentiful. There was a small pond for bathing and drinking. Cherry trees swayed back and forth at the side of the ledge, while forests of pine, oak, cedar, spruce, and maple trees surrounded their area. For the next 12 days, Armand gathered twigs, leaves, moss, dried grass, and bits of molted rabbit and deer fur. Beth would arrange the twigs and leaves to suit her needs. Standing in the nest she would weave together the soft strips of bark Armand had torn from trees, finally lining the cup of the nest with moss and animal fur. On the outside the nest looked like an untidy pile of twigs. The inside cup where the eggs would be laid was a beautifully finished piece of work. Armand and Beth would work all morning and spend the afternoons eating, mating, and resting.

"Our nest is complete, Beth," Armand said sitting side by side in a large oak tree. Beth continued to rub his neck with her beak. "Now all that is missing is the remainder of the clan," he said, pecking her beak.

Chapter 2: Then There Were Nine

BETH REMAINED ON the nest incubating eight mottled green eggs. The brood patch, an almost featherless section of the body, touches the eggs allowing the heat from her body to pass directly to them. Finally, after 19 days of incubation, Dempster, the first-born, was followed by Allie, Berto, Gilroy, Kirkwell, Yago, and Cassandra. Beth and Armand gazed into the nest while eating pieces of shell surrounding the mass of pale pink flesh speckled with tufts of down. One egg remained unhatched.

"Four boys and three girls!" Armand rejoiced strutting back and forth in front of Beth sitting on the nest. "I wonder what the last egg will produce."

"One or the other," Beth mused, as she watched with pride, her handsome mate. She knew the first time he had pursued her that there was no doubt she would be his lifelong partner.

Armand stopped suddenly and looked toward a clump of maple trees. The new leaves of early spring couldn't harbour the enemy sitting on a branch watching them. A wild cawing erupted out of him. The distinct cry, almost a scream, translating into owl, put him on a direct course toward the maples. This cry normally brought every crow within hearing distance but they were too far up the mountain for others to hear. Beth, torn between motherly instincts and her mate took flight also, knowing Armand would be no match on his own for a great horned owl. With both of them in pursuit, the owl left the area.

Beth quickly returned to the nest while Armand circled above making sure the owl was gone then landed on the grassy overhang and heard Beth crying. "What's the matter?" he asked, not sure he wanted to hear the answer.

"The egg has been taken!" Beth was on the verge of hysterics. It was the price she had paid for leaving the nest.

"The others are all accounted for," Armand said, as he quickly did a head count while consoling Beth. Any number of enemies could have taken the egg. Whether it was a snake, raccoon, owl, or eagle, the deed was done. The culprit would remain unknown.

In the days that followed, Beth and Armand tended to the brood. Their eyes were open now and their skin was slightly touched with brown feathers. Days later, their feathers had grown rapidly and so had their appetites. Both parents took turns flying back and forth with insects, worms, and bits of meat torn from carrion, fruit, and berries. The constant clamour for food kept a parent at the nest until the other returned. Any passing predator would be drawn to an easy meal of baby crow.

At the end of four weeks they had most of their feathers. It was time to learn the lessons of life.

Chapter 3: Family Ties/Severed Ties

'Ties that bind us to family form the tightest knots'

THE DAY DAWNED sunny and warm. The clan had matured considerably and was now ready to learn about survival.

"Please come here," Father called to his offspring sitting side by side in the crowded nest. One by one they hopped out of the nest and walked over to where their parents stood.

"Now listen up. I am going to teach you how to hunt and take care of yourselves in a world full of many challenges and mysteries. You must pay attention to everything I say if you want to survive. These lessons are very important. Most have been passed on from generation to generation."

Father looked toward the end of the line-up. "Dempster, pay attention!" he yelled. He watched him peck at Yago's head who was trying hard to listen.

Dempster stopped. "I am," he cawed scratching at the ground with his left foot. He seemed to have no interest in what Father was saying.

"As crows, we have the distinct recognition of being one of the most intelligent birds on earth. I'm not sure who holds the title of being the most intelligent, but I like to think crows rule. Using your intelligence and instincts in all aspects will take you through the many challenges you will encounter. Because life without challenge is no life at all," Father said, passing a loving glance at Mother.

"First, you must learn how to feed yourselves. We are omnivorous and will eat almost anything. Scavengers are what we have been referred to by humans because we eat their road kill, when in fact we are doing them a favour."

"What are humans?" Kirkwell asked.

"Good question, Son. They're odd creatures. Not at all like us, the rulers of the sky. They have skin instead of feathers and walk on two feet and arms with hands instead of wings so they can't fly. Brains? Only if they put them to good use. As our enemy, they take up guns to control our population. Sadly, they feel we are a menace when quite the contrary is true. I'll give you an example of how dumb humans can be. A couple of years ago, numbers of us descended on Metcalf's asparagus field. When he made this discovery, he hired humans to shoot us, which was more of a battle of wits than a test of great skill with their guns. The lookouts sent out a warning as soon as the hunters arrived, sending us airborne in a matter of seconds. There were only a few casualties because our advantage lies in our intelligence, ability to communicate, and working together. We all left the area. And guess what? To Metcalf's dismay, his asparagus didn't grow. One morning, after close examination of the field, he found thousands upon thousands of cutworms. They lie buried during the day but come out at night to eat the roots of young plants. As for the crows' part, we would rise early to feed on the cutworms before they could re-bury themselves. Well, he finally figured out that we were eating the cutworms NOT the asparagus plants and then left us alone. Very cautiously we returned to the field to finish our job. We cleaned up the cutworms and the asparagus crop prospered. You see, what humans consider destructive or scavenging is a matter of survival for us. We have to eat!"

"Now, the first thing we need is a lookout," Father said, looking back and forth at the brood. "In a flock, older, wiser crows are usually posted in strategic positions. They have more experience spotting oncoming danger. There are enough of us to take turns as a lookout while the others eat."

Father knew exactly where to post the lookout. "Watch carefully. There's an oak tree I am heading for which stands much taller than the surrounding trees. It is a vantage point that provides good camouflage making the lookout almost invisible," he said before flying out of sight.

"Where did Father go?" Yago asked as all eyes scanned the area in the direction their father had flown.

"I'm right behind you," he said startling them all. "First lesson. Never, ever let your guard down. Always be aware of your surroundings and know exactly who is entering your area. It could be a matter of life or death. Now, are you ready for your first major flight to the lookout point?"

"Yes Father," they said in unison and proceeded to follow. One by one they perched on a large branch of the oak tree enabling them to see firsthand an overview of their home area.

"Not only can you see our area but no one can see you. Now, who wants to take the first posting?" Father asked, scanning their faces.

"I will," Kirkwell volunteered.

"Thank you Kirkwell. I'm proud of you, Son. At the first sign of danger sound the alarm with your loudest voice." Father let out a loud caw.

Kirkwell drew a deep breath then echoed his father's caw. "Perfect. A chip off the old block, Mother," Father said giving her a loving nudge.

The remainder of the family flew back to their area in search of seeds and insects, each taking their turn as a lookout. Dempster was the last one to take a turn. He was just piercing a juicy slug with his long black beak when his father called him. "It's your turn, Son."

He swallowed down the slug. "I'm on my way, Father."

Dempster landed on the assigned oak branch, taking in a bird's eye view of his family. *I'll be the best lookout this family has ever had. I'm first born and the oldest,* he thought smugly, fidgeting back and forth on the branch. *Kirkwell thinks he's the best. I'll show Father who to be the proudest of. Starting right now.*

He let go of the branch and landed clumsily on the ground below. "And just what do you think you are doing?" he asked, in a loud voice. He watched as a black-capped chickadee continued eating some fallen seeds trying to ignore its unwelcome intruder.

Dempster stood mesmerized as the chickadee continued searching for seeds. "Hey! You little pipsqueak. Can't you see I'm talking to you?"

The chickadee turned and looked Dempster in the eye. "Of course I can see you."

Now that Dempster had its attention, "are you aware who I am?"

"Are you aware of whom I am?" the chickadee retorted.

He didn't know what to make of this fearless little interloper. "I am Dempster the crow, firstborn of the great Armand and the lovely Beth. I have been assigned to keep intruders like you as far away from OUR area as possible. Now get!"

The chickadee had very little patience for such a silly bird but took the time to explain that he is a sentinel of the forest. "I send out an alert cry to any bird or creature that is willing to heed this as a warning of imminent danger with a special call that could save your life one day. It sounds like this," the chickadee cried before flying off.

Dempster watched as the chickadee flew off into the woods. "Bingo! I took care of that little pest."

"That you did," a voice from behind him said.

He turned around quickly. "Father! You scared the wits out of me!"

"Dempster, you were supposed to remain in the tree and send out a warning alerting the family of any potential danger. Do you have any idea of how much danger there was to our family when you deserted the lookout post?"

"But Father. I thought you would be proud of me for saving the family."

Father shook his head slowly and sighed. "Son, a chickadee is not an enemy of the crow or any other creature of the forest for that matter. They are very helpful and do warn of potential danger with their loud cries. And like it said, `one day one may save your life'. If you had been paying attention to the lesson I gave on enemies, this would not have happened."

"But father."

His father raised his wing instantly stopping his protest. "I want you to fly back to the others and wait for me."

Like his father, Dempster was not one to back down. "But what about my lookout time?" he said, knowing who would be taking his place.

"Kirkwell is already in position. Now go back with the others," Father said before flying off.

Dempster looked up to where his brother sat proudly scanning the area. *Kirkwell, always Kirkwell,* he said to himself before taking off.

Summer on Magassus Mountain was perfect for the crow family. With just the right amount of sunshine and rain, the family continued to grow and prosper together. One sunny day, Father summoned his brood to the pond. "Today we are going to celebrate the wind. The air currents up beyond that steep cliff over there are perfect for some flying tricks," he said pointing up.

"How do you know that father?" Berto questioned.

"Good question, Son. While all of you were filling your faces this morning, I was flying over our territory searching for predators. In doing so, I found the wind currents quite favourable for what I would like to show you."

"But how do you know they were favourable?" Berto persisted.

Father decided immediately that this son was going to be very successful in his life. He questioned everything he was unsure of and waited patiently for the answer. "Instinct, Son. That and a sense of adventure for the unknown. Hopefully you all have these qualities well inbred."

"Having such a great father also helps."

Father breathed in deeply. *Another complete success.* "Why thank you Kirkwell."

Dempster rolled his eyes skyward. *Brown noser. I'll show him.* "What does instinct mean father?"

Father turned toward him. *Maybe there's hope after all.* "Another good question, Son. It's a feeling deep inside that just seems to happen causing one to respond in a particular way, often without a specific reason."

"Like the time I left the lookout post?"

Father looked toward the nest. "Yes and no. You had been told not to leave your post."

"But my instincts were telling me something different."

That doesn't surprise me, his father thought, but didn't say. "Beth, help me out here."

Mother turned to Dempster. "It's more of a feeling from inside you, than something that's learned. One just seems to know and reacts accordingly."

Father looked at his mate. "Your mother always seems to know how to say the right thing."

She returned his loving gaze. "Instinct my dear, instinct."

"Now, your mother and I will show you the marvellous things a pair of wings can do. Enjoy the show," Father called out before flying straight up with Mother close behind. Once air borne, their parents took turns swooping, whirling, and turning completely over.

"Wow! Look at Mother and Father," cooed Gilroy. "I wish I could do that."

"Me too," Kirkwell said as they all looked skyward.

Dempster looked upward periodically. "Being the oldest, I'm too busy watching for predators."

"Holy mackerel! They're falling out of the sky," Gilroy exclaimed as each parent folded its wings and began falling.

The family froze in place watching and wondering what would become of their parents, but to their surprise, they began spinning upward once again.

"That was awesome!" Cassandra said, as their parents glided back down to them. "Can we try it now?"

"You sure can," Mother said.

The others had congregated around their parents. Dempster walked over to join them. "I stood watch while you were doing your stunts," he said proudly.

"That's good Son, but your mother and I had a very clear view of our territory at all times."

"I thought you would be proud Father," he said clawing at the ground with his left foot.

"I am, Dempster. One can never be too cautious. Now, let's all head for the sky," Father yelled, taking wing with each member of the family close behind.

They spent their time dodging and weaving through the sky until Father signalled it was time to go back home.

Once the brood settled for the night, Mother and Father sat side by side watching the sunset below the highest peak of Magassus.

"It was a good day," Father sighed, moving closer to his mate.

"They all enjoyed themselves and will sleep well tonight," she said wearily.

Armand wasn't as tired and wanted to talk. "Beth, I'm concerned about Dempster. He never seems to listen or pay attention like the others. It's like he is off in his own world most of the time."

Beth held back a yawn. "He just wants to please, especially you. Unlike the others, he needs continual praise no matter how small the task. You must be patient with him Armand. And don't lose your temper."

Armand sighed. "He frustrates me. The others don't need half as much attention as Dempster. He seems so different from the rest."

Beth turned toward her mate shaking her head slowly. "You once told me that being different was good. You were so different from the rest of the pack. That's what I love about you most," Beth cooed rubbing her beak behind his head.

Armand slowly moved his head from side to side. "I just hope things work out for him."

"Dempster will be just fine. Good night, Armand."

Somehow, Armand wasn't as convinced. "Good night, Beth."

The next morning shortly after sunrise, Father called the family together. "Today, we are going on an adventure. We are going to fly off the mountain and into the valley for our breakfast. How does fresh duckling or gosling sound? How about fresh loon eggs? It's time you all learned how to raid waterfowl nests, or any bird's nest for that matter. Are you ready?" The family nodded in unison then fell into place behind their father as he took wing.

The pack flew down Magassus into a forest of mostly evergreen trees. Perching on a great white pine, Father spoke very quietly. "There are hundreds of nests in these woods."

"How do you know that?" Berto whispered.

"Crows know the location of every nest in their territory, long before the eggs are in it, by stalking the area while the nests are being constructed." In Armand's younger years, he spent many early spring days, as his father had, quietly scouting the forests and marshes for birds returning to their nesting areas. He discovered at an early age that most birds or their offspring return to the same area making his task of nest hunting much easier. He would sit silently in the budding greenery of deciduous trees watching, making a mental note of each nest location.

Now he was passing this important information on to his young. "You must always know where your next meal is. I want you to be very quiet and wait here for me."

The brood watched closely as he flew to a birch tree and in one quick swoop he grabbed one of the morning dove babies then returned to a nearby branch and proceeded to tear it apart. Silently, the rest of the clan joined him, sharing in the catch.

They left the forest and flew down toward a small lake at the base of the mountain landing in the trees near the water's edge. Quietly, they sat watching and waiting for the geese and ducks to leave their nests. They were never far from their nests during these much-needed breaks. Yet far enough to give the crows an opportunity to raid their nests of eggs and small hatchlings.

The crow family quickly descended on the nests and began pecking at the eggs expertly breaking the spotted shells and consuming their contents while distraught geese and ducks sounded the alarm, trying in vain to attack the flock. With most of the eggs cracked and the contents consumed, Father let out a loud caw signalling the family to take to the skies. The geese and ducks surveyed their nests of broken eggshells and dismembered hatchlings, crying out loudly in the crows' wake.

The pack continued flying until Father sighted a fairly large object at the side of a road. He began his descent landing near a dead cat.

"Looks pretty fresh," Mother said gazing at the lifeless animal.

Before feasting on the carrion, Father commented on how smoothly the waterfowl raid went. "The main lesson today was that there is safety in numbers. The geese and ducks were in no position to deal with the raid. They know that a pack of hungry crows will have its way. It is virtually unstoppable," Father said confidently.

He turned toward the black and white spotted cat that had the misfortune of crossing the highway at the wrong time. "Dig in. It's almost time to go back home."

The days were beginning to shorten as summer wound down. Light mist would descend on their area in the early morning hours. One morning the fog was so thick they could not see the pond.

"Father, what is happening?" Allie cried.

"Where is our pond?" Dempster asked half asleep.

"Where is everybody?" Gilroy yelled.

"It is okay everyone," Father replied calmly from somewhere in the fog. "We're experiencing a foggy morning. Now that the days are getting shorter, we have seen some misty mornings." He looked around the area trying to locate his family. "But this is out and out fog."

"What is fog?" they asked in unison.

It was all quite eerie to say the least. Father could hear them but had no idea where they were. "Droplets of water vapour suspended in the air near the ground. It seems to happen more in the fall as the air gets colder."

He encouraged them to stay put because the fog was so thick. "It will dissipate as the sun climbs higher in the sky."

"Does this mean we are fogbound?" Dempster asked from his perch.

"Looks like it. We are certainly unable to go anywhere," Father said. Mother finally located her mate beside the pond.

By midday the fog finally lifted, leaving in its wake a warm, sunny, early fall day. The brood were searching for food or bathing in the pond when Father called them together near the nest. "Your mother and I are very proud of all of you. Now that you have matured nicely, you will need to choose a lifelong mate. This will guarantee future generations of crows. Your mother and I are going to demonstrate how to attract a partner. I, of course, will demonstrate the male's part so pay attention sons. First, make yourself look handsome, important, and as attractive as possible. Like this."

Father held his head up proudly, puffed out his feathers, spreading out his wings and tail feathers. He began strutting around Mother bobbing his head up and down making a series of rattling noises followed by a soft coo-coo. He then took to the air whirling, diving, and flashing close by her. Mother pretended to be completely unaware of her suitor. She did not look directly at him, instead turning her head then flying off a short distance with Father following her.

They quickly flew back to the brood. Father continued with the lesson. "If she has no interest, look for another mate. Sometimes your first choice may not be the right choice. Even in my case, I have to admit, I was beginning to wonder about your mother. She showed little, if any, interest in my advances in the beginning. Turns out she was just playing hard to get."

Father thought back to his experience with Beth. "And sometimes you will have a competition if two males want to court the same female and she shows no definite preference." Again his thoughts wandered back to his experience. "This means war to us males who know what we want. It is exactly what happened when I was pursuing your mother."

Beth began recanting what happened that day. "Your father put up a heroic fight. He and the other male took off clashing in mid-air trying to rise above one another, battering with wings and bills before falling to the ground.

The fight continued as they rolled about until the weaker suitor finally gave up and left."

The brood turned and looked at Father standing proudly with his head held high as Mother continued. "I watched the fight from a tree branch, hoping your father would win. I had my eye on him also."

Armand stopped posing and turned toward her. "I had no idea."

"I knew exactly who I wanted to spend the rest of my life with the moment I laid eyes on you."

Armand drew a deep breath expanding his chest fully. "Now that's love."

Mother demonstrated what the female does to show her acceptance. She squatted in front of Armand, half raising her wings, spreading her tail feathers and quivering. She then opened her bill and made small chirping sounds, at which time, Father presented her with a piece of carrion he had hidden beside a rock. This is the ultimate show of affection.

Father turned toward the males. "It is also the responsibility of the male to find and defend a nesting area such as the one you have grown up in."

Mother took her place beside her mate. "I hope you are all as fortunate as your father and I and find the perfect mate."

"Aw shucks Beth," Armand replied lowering his head and clawing at the ground with his left foot.

Early one morning, Father returned from his morning flying exercise and called the family together. He stood patiently as the mature brood gathered beside the pond. "This is the time I have been waiting for. Migration has begun. Down in the valley many flocks of crows are gathering to roost near easy food sources as they begin their flight further south. It is time for us to join them." He was just about to give them further instruction.

"What! Leave the mountain? Our home!" Dempster exclaimed.

Father was unprepared for his outcry. Migration was a natural part of a crow's yearly cycle. "Of course we have to leave our home. Weren't you listening to your mother and me when we talked about finding a mate? You have all matured enough to begin your search for a mate and establish territories of your own. This part of your lives on Magassus Mountain is just the first step."

Dempster continued to argue. "This area is perfect for all of us. We can stay here together as a family forever. We have everything we need right here."

Father stood speechless trying to think of what to say next.

"Well I'm ready to move on," Kirkwell interjected. He couldn't believe his brother would think he wanted to stay. "I don't want to live here on the mountain forever. I want to explore the world. Meet other crows. Find a mate."

In unison, the others nodded in agreement. Dempster could not believe his ears. "Well I am staying put!" He stamped his left foot driving home the point.

Mother looked horrified. "Dempster, you can't stay here on the mountain by yourself. It would be so lonely. Don't you want to explore this wonderful world of ours? There are so many different places to live. And what about finding a mate and starting a family of your own?"

Dempster had little interest in finding a mate. "I'm happy here with you and Father and the rest of my siblings. I don't want to leave the mountain."

"You have to leave. It's, it's, the 'Law of Nature'," Father exclaimed in frustration.

Beth turned sharply toward Armand, wondering where he was going with this one.

Denpster looked toward his father. "'The Law of Nature', what's that?"

Father thought quickly. "It's a law that says all creatures must leave their mother and father to make a life of their own. We gave you life, now it is up to you to live it to the fullest," he said in one breath.

Beth had never been more proud of her mate and she was sure Dempster would change his mind.

"Well we can break protocol and remain together. `Law of Nature.' Sounds dumb to me," Dempster replied.

"What! And go against the `Law of Nature'?" Father yelled. "I don't think so. Why, we'd be the laughing stock of every crow for miles around." Not that he gave a hoot.

Dempster looked his father in the eye. "Well I'm not leaving the mountain."

Father stood his ground. "Suit yourself. But you are making a huge mistake. In the end, you will be nothing but a lonely, sad, old cackling crow, Son," he replied before flying off.

They all stood silently watching as Father cut a swath through the cloudy sky.

Mother walked over to Dempster. "Just give your decision some more thought, Son. Your father is right. You will be very lonely." Not to mention the dangers he could encounter as a single crow. "I love you very much."

He didn't notice the tears in his mother's eyes as she flew toward the lookout tree and found Armand perched on a large branch.

"I hope you spoke to Dempster and got him to change his mind. Of all the stupid things I've ever heard."

"I have asked him to reconsider his decision and hopefully he will."

Armand shuffled sideways on the branch. "He is so headstrong that one. I doubt he will change his mind."

"I wonder where he gets that from." Beth whispered quietly.

"It is one thing to be headstrong and another to be stupid. I can't believe he would want to live here alone on the mountain."

Beth looked at Armand. "And who brought us here in the first place? You didn't feel that way when you wanted to establish 'our own unique territory'."

Armand thought back to the mob of crows in the cornfield and surrounding forests. "That was different. I wanted to get away from the flock. It was just too crowded."

Beth sighed. "Hopefully Dempster will give more thought to his conclusion of remaining on Magassus."

"And if he doesn't?" Armand said, shifting on the branch.

During the next few days, the family took turns trying to convince Dempster to migrate with them. "I'm not going!" Dempster said, standing his ground.

Stubbornly, Father stood his. "I guess this is good-bye then. You are making a big mistake, Son." Father stood watching as the rest of the clan took turns saying good-bye.

"Please come with us," Mother begged.

"I'm staying," he said adamantly.

"Dempster, please. You are breaking my heart," she sobbed.

"Come Mother. We have a long flight and the others have started on ahead," Father said, wrapping his wing around her gently encouraging her to fly. "Good luck Son. We love you," Father stammered before taking wing.

Dempster watched as his parents flew away to join his siblings until they were no more than tiny specks in the turquoise sky. "They'll be back," he said smugly. "They'll be back."

Chapter 4: The Art of Being Alone

LATE FALL SNOW had begun and the seemingly endless flocks of migrating birds had finally ceased. The branches of trees that were once leafy swayed naked and vulnerable to gusty mountain winds. A hibernation silence engulfed the area leaving those remaining to brave the elements, susceptible to nature's wrath.

Dempster scrounged around the rocks where he had hidden food and began pecking at a frozen piece of carrion before moving on to where he had stashed some seeds. He had been smart enough to begin storing food long before the snows began. But as the snow deepened, it was more difficult to find these hidden morsels and he had to spend a great deal of time digging with his beak and claws through snow that had drifted up against the rocks.

Dempster, now fully grown, was closer in size to his cousin the raven. At 52 centimeters in length, he was definitely a force to be reckoned with. But only in his mind. The mountain, especially this portion, was his and he vowed to do everything in his power to keep it that way. After he had finished eating, he began walking around the area making sure he was alone. He glanced toward the nest. "Well look at that," he said, noting the footprints he had left behind in the snow.

He flew over to a flat area nearby and began making designs in the newly fallen snow. But as quickly as he made the prints, the wind blew them away. He stood gazing at the nest area and thought of his family and how life on the mountain had been so complete. He was on his own and had given up on the notion that his family would return.

Angrily, he stomped the snow then flew over to the nest and rearranged some of the twigs so that a wall of sticks surrounded the inner cup. Bitterly, he looked up and watched as cold, grey clouds swallowed the sun. Thankful for the overhang above the nest, he hunkered down as winter's fury began to change the landscape.

Survival on the mountain proved to be a major challenge, but a determined Dempster was up for it. There were tense moments when food was scarce. He had depleted his food stashes and quickly realized that the only way he would survive was to venture away from his area. He flew to another area of the mountain and sat for hours in huge evergreens that camouflaged his presence. During this time, he discovered how the food chain works.

From his vantage point, he watched a cougar silently stalking a small herd of deer keeping its distance. Dempster shivered in excitement as he watched the graceful but powerful cat move in for the kill quickly taking down the youngest or weakest of the herd. The remainder scattered in all directions running for their lives.

Dempster would sit quietly awaiting his turn, watching as the cougar had its feed then moved the remainder of the uneaten carcass behind some rocks or trees for future meals. Once the cougar had moved on, Dempster would quickly fly down and feast cautiously on the leftovers. Tirelessly, he would fly back and forth with bits of meat to hide near his nest for easy meals.

He spent windless winter days drawing abstract creations in the snow with his feet and beak. His artistic creations froze in place during the cold nights. On clear sunny days, he would soar alone on the wind currents as he once did with his family. Though it was not the same, he still found the experience exhilarating.

One clear, moonless night as he settled into the nest he looked up at the sky and was astounded at how clear and bright the stars were. They were so close he could almost touch them. He thought about his family and his father's explanation on how each star was different and unique.

"They are different, like me," he said softly as his eyes scanned the sky. He couldn't understand what was wrong with being different. On occasion, he had overheard his father say to Mother that he wasn't like the rest of the brood. She would say 'it was okay to be different'. At times like this, he was glad he was different and had decided to remain on Magassus.

He continued gazing up at the stars creating a poem:

The Star

"When you look in the sky,
you'll probably not see,
two stars alike,
they are different like me.

Some shine brighter as they wink way up there.
Some are part of a group, really not fair.
But the one on its own that twinkles so free,
is the one that stands out,
it's different like me.

This star must work harder than most in the sky.
Competition is fierce,
it really must try.
Its strong inner self is how it gets by.
The reward will be worth it.
For it will catch your eye.

When you encounter someone not like you.
They may have to work harder or longer times two.

Remember the star so high in the sky.
The one that stands alone will catch your eye.
It may not be the brightest or the largest you'll
see
But it holds its own, because it's different like
me."

"Yes, that about sums me up," Dempster said with pride. "The Star. That's what I am. Everyone will come to know that about me." Content with his new creation, he repeated it to himself again and again until he fell asleep. He was so proud of his poem, *The Star*, became his nightly mantra before bed.

Water at the edge of the pond was beginning to appear as the sun grew stronger and warmer in the early spring days that followed Dempster's first winter on Magassus Mountain. Wild flowers sprouted as the last traces of snow evaporated. As the trees began budding, the mountain animals came to life reclaiming territories given up during hibernation. Flocks of birds filled the once vacant skies as they headed back to summer breeding grounds.

Dempster walked about assessing his area making sure his territory had withstood the winter and thankfully it had. "I can live on my own. I don't need anybody. This is my mountain and my life," he said proudly, strutting back and forth near the pond.

"I am Dempster the crow. The Star. What do you think you are doing?" he yelled when a chipmunk came to the pond for a drink, interrupting his speech. The chipmunk ran off when Dempster flapped his wings. "And stay away," he yelled.

"This is my home." He puffed out his feathers and gazed at his handsome reflection at the edge of pond. "Yes, life is good."

Chapter 5: Beatriss

JUST BEFORE THE first light of dawn, Dempster was disturbed by something moving on the ground in front of his nest. Directing his eyes toward the noise, he could not locate the source. *I must be hearing things* he thought stretching slowly as the new day began.

The once bare aspen, oak, cherry, and poplar trees were turning green with new leaf growth. Grass, dandelions, yellow columbine, glacier lilies, and cow parsnip coloured the once barren landscape in various shades of yellow. The sun shone brightly bringing much needed warmth to this area of the mountain as Dempster bathed in the pond.

Walking out of the water, he spotted a young snowshoe hare grazing in some nearby grass. "Hey! Who invited you?" he called out, shaking the water off his body.

The hare continued eating unperturbed by his presence. "Well I never," Dempster mumbled advancing to the grassy patch. A strange noise stopped him in his tracks.

As he proceeded, the noise became louder. It was a sound he had never heard before. He had no idea where it was coming from. His instincts told him something was amiss. Dempster slowly backed away while keeping an eye on the little brown hare. The noise ceased. He discovered that a few steps forward would trigger the strange noise.

"I could have some fun with this..." he stopped mid-sentence and watched as the hare's hind legs turned up and out sideways before disappearing in the tall grass. "What the heck?" Everything seemed a little too quiet. "I had better return to my nest and think about this," he said, backing away slowly.

Back at the nest, he tried in vain to remember all the predators that his father had warned him about. "Maybe he just hopped away and I didn't notice. No, I was standing right there watching. I will wait a while then fly over and check it out."

Dempster could tell by the position of the sun that enough time had elapsed. *Time to investigate.* He flew to a nearby tree to survey the grassy patch. "There isn't hide nor hare of that little pest," he observed chuckling at his own joke. "That's a good one. What would I expect from The Star," he laughed thinking how intelligent he is. He flew down to the ground to take a closer look. Somehow, the hare had disappeared without a trace.

Dempster began pecking the ground for insects and seeds making his way over to a large rock where he had stashed bits of carrion during the winter. He noticed a black and white banded object with a horny section on the end of it. He picked it up in his beak and pulled back. A tug-of-war ensued yanking him off his feet.

"What in the world?" he yelled. He regained his footing and looked toward the rock. The object had disappeared, but the noise he had heard earlier this morning was louder than ever.

"We'll see about this," he said walking around the rock focusing on the noise. "What do you think you are doing?" he questioned in an authoritative tone.

The noise continued.

"Do you have any idea where you are? This is my territory and no one gets into it, EVER!" he bellowed, holding his head high. There was still no response, just the noise.

"Cat got your tongue?" Dempster chuckled. "I ate a cat once," he said as his mind wandered back to the family feast.

"Well, seeing you've decided not to speak to me. Do you have any idea who I am? I am Dempster the crow, firstborn of the great Armand and the lovely Beth. I own this mountain area and you are trespassing!" he said moving forward while trying to see what was making the noise.

"And do you have any idea who I am?" she asked stopping him in his tracks. "I am Beatrissssssss, the diamondback rattlesnake," she continued, coiling up tighter, swaying her head from side to side.

"Beatrisssssss?" Dempster mimicked. "Sounds like you have been eating too many poppy seeds."

"One should never make fun of those who are different from themselves," she hissed. "That difference could cost you your life."

"Yeah, well I'm not afraid of anything," Dempster retorted.

"Still not afraid?" Beatriss asked striking out from her coiled position.

"Hey! What are you doing?" Dempster cried losing his balance.

"You should have some fear," she said circling quickly around him.

"I can hardly see you!" he wailed.

"That's because I am well camouflaged. See how well I blend in with the dirt and rocks. This is where my ability lies," she said, striking at him once again.

"Your ability?" he questioned fearfully, narrowly avoiding the strike. It was all he could do to concentrate on her whereabouts.

"My ability to move in quickly for the kill, poisoning you with my venom, then retreating while the toxins spread inside of you," she hissed. Beatriss opened her mouth wide revealing a large fang with smaller fangs behind it. "You see. I'm different, like you."

"Did you use your venom to kill the hare?" he cried, as Beatriss began circling him once again.

"That hare didn't know what hit him. Now are you afraid?" she whispered.

"Yes! Help!" he screamed. "Please stop circling me."

"One should always have a little fear, silly crow. It keeps the senses alive and hopefully, in your case, some sensibility," she cautioned then quickly slithered away.

Dempster caught his breath. "Well I never," he huffed. "Fear? Sensibility? What does some stupid old rattlesnake know? This is my mountain and I'm still not afraid of anything!" he yelled, walking toward his nest on trembling legs.

Each morning, just before daylight Dempster would hear something moving on the ground in front of his nest. "Beatriss, is that you?" he would call out. There was no answer.

Dempster went about his daily routine of bathing, eating, and flying exercises. One day, as he was doing one of his art creations in the dirt, he noticed a smaller rock sitting on a much larger rock. "That wasn't there before," he said, flying over to the area and landing in a tree close by.

"Well, well, there's Beatrisssssss the rattlesnake." She lay sunning herself on the rock, well aware of Dempster's presence. He flew down and landed close by her. "How come there is no noise?" he questioned.

"You mean like this?" she hissed shaking her tail vigorously and coiling herself in a split second to the striking position.

"Yeah," Dempster said, stepping back. "That's quite a getup," he said nervously.

"This `getup' as you so boldly call it, is my way of surviving."

"I see."

"Do you? Do you `see' that I could have killed you the moment you made the mistake of landing on this rock?"

"First of all, it is not a mistake that I landed on this rock and secondly, I own it," he replied belligerently.

Beatriss shook her head. "You don't own this rock."

Dempster puffed out his feathers. "I beg to differ. I own this rock and every rock around here."

"My dear Dempster," she replied patiently. "You are not alone on this mountain. There are all kinds of creatures both on the ground and in the sky that also have territory on Magassus. The very least you can do is learn how to share and respect this because it isn't going to change."

"Well I see things differently," he replied adamantly. "When my family left me, I decided I didn't need or want anybody around me. I like being on my own and that means no one around, including you."

Beatriss slithered up close to him. "Have you ever wondered why I have not killed you and eaten you?"

"Maybe," he replied feeling her warm breath caress his face before stepping back.

"Because you are young, naive and inexperienced in life's many challenges." *Also very cocky.*

"And I suppose you know all about this stuff?" he cut in rudely.

"Enough to know that respect for others' differences is a major factor for survival."

"Ha!" he exclaimed. "I know how to survive. How do you think I got through my first winter here? It wasn't until creatures like you started coming out of the woodwork that all my troubles began."

He just doesn't get it. "Do you want to know how I got on this mountain?" she questioned.

Dempster moved his head back and forth in boredom. "Yeah, whatever. Where did you come from?"

Beatriss wondered why she was trying to get through to the most belligerent creature she had ever encountered and not killed and eaten. Frustrated she asked him to look skyward toward the top of the mountain. "See that large bird circling way up there? Do you have any idea what it is?"

She was getting weary and didn't wait for his reply. "It's a golden eagle. Her name is Celeste, short for celestial. As she circles above, she is watching every move we make here on the rock bantering back and forth."

Dempster looked skyward and watched as Celeste circled in the heavens. *There's no way she can see us from way up there. Probably just another Beatriss fable.* He was more interested in how she got here. "So what's that got to do with your presence here on my mountain?"

"She put me here," Beatriss hissed indignantly.

"No kidding," he replied.

Beatriss ignored his smart-ass tone. "I used to live at the base of Magassus. One day I was looking for my next meal. I was so intent on finding food, I let my guard down. Before I realized what was happening, Celeste had me in her talons flying up toward her nesting area. Suddenly, a flock of ravens roosting on a mountain cliff nearby began attacking her. Relentlessly they dove and swerved at her until she was too weak to fly and hold on to me. With her own survival at stake, she released me and I fell through the air. A large evergreen broke my fall. I was cut and bruised but alive. Regaining my senses, I made my way down the tree to the nearest boulder. Slithering under, I remained there until I was healed." She focused on Dempster hoping he'd listened very carefully to what she had just told him.

"What does my name mean?" he asked.

Beatriss could not believe his question. Did he even listen to what she had just said? "One who judges," she replied exasperated.

"No kidding." He thought back to the day his family left him and wondered briefly if he had judged wrongly.

"Perhaps you are thinking about when your family left you?" Beatriss said quietly.

Dempster didn't hold back. "Yes I am! They abandoned me! I wanted to stay on the mountain and live happily with them forever."

Beatriss moved in closer to him. "They didn't abandon you. You chose to stay behind."

"Are you saying I used bad judgment in staying?" he said defensively, thinking about what his name means.

Beatriss had had enough for today. "Time will tell," she replied, slithering off the rock.

"Hey! Wait a minute. How did you know all this?" he called after her.

There was no reply. He was getting used to the silence. Dempster flew over to the pond and watched as Celeste continued circling high above the mountain. *There is no way she can see me way down here. Stupid snake, what does she know.*

The days were nice and warm now. Though Dempster continued to keep most intruders at bay, he did not question Beatriss's presence anymore. In fact, he found her to be a good mentor and surprisingly he had developed a great respect for her. Beatriss on the other hand, found Dempster to be more than she could handle. However, she was now able to go about her daily business without too much interference from him.

One day, Dempster tried in vain to locate Beatriss. Their paths had not crossed for a few days. He would call her name but there was never an answer. "I wonder where she is," he said searching around some of the rocks he knew she hid under to avoid the hot summer sun. He was just about to give up when he noticed something between two large dark grey boulders. With trembling legs he moved cautiously toward it.

"Beatriss! There you are! I have been looking for you for days," he stopped talking and stared at her. Her eyes were clouded over and she did not move.

"Oh no! She's dead!" he cried backing away from her. "She's dead! She's dead!" he cried before flying back to his nest. He was so upset he remained there until the following morning.

Just before daylight, he heard a strange noise moving on the ground in front of his nest. "Beatriss. Is that you?"

There was no answer.

Dempster waited until the sun was high in the sky to finally get up enough nerve to return to the place where he had found Beatriss. He walked quietly over to the rocks and looked down.

"She's gone!" he cried looking up toward Celeste's area of the mountain. She was nowhere in sight. He looked back at the space between the rocks.

"Oh my goodness! All that is left of Beatriss is her skin." He pulled out the long piece of skin that used to be Beatriss and could barely hold it in his beak he was crying so hard.

"Well, well. It looks like 'the star' has got feelings after all," Beatriss hissed.

He spit the skin out of his mouth. "There you are! But, but, I thought you were ..."

"Dead?" she filled in.

"Yes!"

She stretched out to her full length exposing a new yellow-bordered, light-centered black diamond skin. "Quite the contrary. It was time for me to shed my skin."

Dempster was confused. He had never heard of such a thing. "Well you looked dead to me!"

Beatriss proceeded to explain the process. "About ten days before shedding my skin, I become listless and stop eating. My eyes cloud over. Because I cannot see, I must go into hiding. I secrete oil that loosens my old skin and then peel it off. I start pushing the skin off at my jaw by rubbing against a rough surface. By moving against rocks, logs or tree branches, I literally crawl right out of it."

Dempster rolled his eyes skyward. "How often is this going to happen?"

"Three to four times a year."

"You could have told me," he said testily, reverting back to the Dempster she knew.

"And ruin the chance to witness firsthand that you aren't as cold as you make yourself out to be. That you do have feelings," she replied.

As usual, it was as if he didn't hear a word she said. "How did you know I am `the star'?" he asked curiously.

Beatriss looked him in the eye like she did every time she wanted to make sure he got the message. "Here's something you don't know about me. I am nocturnal. So take heed. You never know where I will be."

Dempster watched as Beatriss slithered away. *She must hear me recite `the star' at night before bed.* "So, did you like my poem?"

"It's different, like you," she called back before disappearing under a large boulder.

"Hey! Wait a minute. Don't we have some catching up to do? I was worried about you." The rustling of leaves on the trees was all he heard.

Pairs of animals and birds on the mountain were giving birth to their young. It reminded Dempster of his family when they were together in this very territory. The bitterness rose inside of him as he watched busy, happy families getting on with their lives. *Just as long as they stay away from me,* he thought, daring any of them to venture too close.

Chapter 6: Celeste 'of the sky'

CELESTE AND HER mate returned to the same nesting site on Magassus Mountain year after year, constructing a new nest on top of the old one. They transported sticks two inches in diameter and up to six feet long in their talons from the lower forested areas then position them with their beaks in layers. Moss, feathers, fur, and lichen were used to line the nest. This year's nest was 1.8 meters in diameter and 1.5 meters high.

Celeste remained on the nest incubating two blotched brown eggs until they hatched. Once hatched, her mate hunted for food to bring back to her, so she could feed the chicks. She remained at or near the nest until the downy young began to feather before she resumed hunting for food with her mate.

Like most golden eagles, Celeste was a dark brown colour, and could be identified by the light brown, almost golden feathers on the top of her head and the back of her neck.

Her life-long mate, though smaller in size, was identical.

Although well covered in feathers after only eight weeks, the eaglets remained near the nest. Even after they were fully grown, the eaglets would remain near the nest so their parents could feed them.

Golden Eagles are by far, the largest and most magnificent of all eagles with few enemies. They have excellent hearing but they hunt by sight. Their extraordinary eyesight allows them to see both forward and sideways enabling their huge brown eyes to see a ground squirrel from 350 meters up in the air. Once spotted, an eagle does not take its eyes off its prey. The eagle folds its wings and dives at high speed coming suddenly upon its prey of jackrabbit, marmot, and even larger mammals when food is scarce. They are able to pluck ducks, geese, and grouse in flight out of the air. When striking, the eagle clutches its prey in its feet piercing the surprised victim with its long, needle-sharp talons, usually causing instant death.

Celeste took advantage of the updrafts of warm air this bright sunny day. A wingspan of seven feet allowed her to soar, seemingly motionless in the sky, while her eyes fixed on the slopes below for any movement. The eaglets were perched on the side of the nest watching as their mother floated effortlessly in the sky not too far from them.

In a split second, Celeste folded her wings and dove out of sight.

Chapter 7: The Star

'its strong inner self is how it gets by'

THE DAY DAWNED sunny and warm, as it had for many days in a row. Dempster decided to do some necessary repairs to his nest now that the days were beginning to shorten. After a quick bath in the pond, he flew into some nearby woods and tore away some birch bark from a dead tree. By the time he arrived back at his nest, a young lamb was grazing in the grass near the pond.

Dempster dropped the bark and flew over to the lamb landing on its back causing it to bolt away in fear. He continued to fly after it. "And stay away!" he yelled, preparing to swoop at it once more.

He quickly changed his mind as a big horned sheep heard the lamb's distressing cry and quickly came to its rescue. Dempster changed course and watched from a tree as the pair moved silently away from the area.

"They meant you no harm," Beatriss said from the large rock where she was sunning herself.

Dempster turned and looked toward her. "Well I don't want them around my mountain."

Beatriss watched as Dempster landed beside her on the rock. Once she had his attention she spoke. "Have you ever watched ants in a colony?"

"No, I haven't watched ants in a colony," he said sarcastically nodding his head from side to side with each word.

His attitude didn't surprise her as she continued speaking. "When you disrupt their nests, they gather up their eggs and food and move elsewhere to start again."

"What do ants have to do with big horned sheep?"

"Like the ants, when you disrupt any mountain creature they just move on. But they are still on 'your' mountain. They are just out of your sight range."

Dempster looked over to the area where the lamb had been. "If they are dumb enough to come back I'll be waiting."

Beatriss looked him in the eye. "You must learn to share the mountain. There is more than enough space. Don't you understand that these animals contribute to your very existence here on Magassus and one day could save your life?"

"All I understand is that they are just another disruption in my life on my mountain."

Beatriss shook her head in frustration. "What about a food source? Did you feed on the carcasses of those less fortunate to survive the hard winters on the mountain?"

Dempster thought of the number of times he followed the cougars who took down the young and fragile animals that wandered with the herds of sheep and deer. "Of course I did." *I would have starved otherwise.* "The point is, I can fly to all my food sources."

"Isn't it much easier having your food sources close by so you don't have to travel far?"

Dempster thought about the cold winter months and the numerous trips back and forth transporting meat from dead carcasses. *But I didn't have anything better to do. It's how I kept myself occupied. It's none of her business.* "How come you know so much?" he asked sarcastically. "Since when are you such an authority? You spend your winters tucked in the ground below the frost line."

"Mostly instinct. The rest I filled in by listening carefully to those more experienced and knowledgeable than myself. Age does bring wisdom. One would be very clever to listen to those we consider old or outdated," she sighed.

"Well I don't care. This is my mountain and everything uninvited will be dealt with."

"Dempster, why must you always argue?" she asked in exasperation. *He just isn't normal and I doubt he ever will be.* "I've got to get out of the sun," Beatriss said beginning to move.

"Why is it whenever I have something to say, you have to leave? Why can't you listen to me for a change? No one ever wants to hear what I have to say. Maybe I have something to say," he rambled.

"We have been on this rock far too long." Beatriss knew the longer they remained on the rock the more of a target they were. Her skin blended in with the surface of the boulder but Dempster's large black body would be easily seen by any predator. She turned toward him. "I'm listening."

Dempster puffed out his feathers. "I am as strong as this rock and I don't need anybody, including you. Do you understand how strong I am in my mind and body?"

Beatriss looked at him kindly. "Dear Dempster. It is okay to be hard as a rock, but be able to crumble once in a while. It's good for your soul."

"What's that got to do with me?"

"Dempster, for the last time, you must come to terms with yourself about sharing the mountain. Otherwise, you will be in continual conflict not only with those around you but within yourself. Constant turmoil has a way of eating away at oneself, until all that is left is a gaping hole."

"I will not … What the …!" he cried, as Beatriss lunged at him sending him tumbling backward off the rock.

Somewhat dazed, he looked up in horror as Celeste captured Beatriss in her talons then ascended skyward, as the chickadees cried out their loud warnings. Dempster lay there in a disheveled heap watching as Celeste carried a limp Beatriss toward the top of the mountain then out of sight. He let out a bloodcurdling scream then flew over to his nest where he remained for several days reliving the horror that unfolded in front of him again, and again.

"Beatriss saved my life," he cried, thinking of how she lunged at him just before Celeste captured her. "I was the eagle's target."

Fits of panic came in waves filled with tears. "She wanted to get off of the rock because we were easy targets but I had to go on and on. She would still be alive if wasn't for me. How did she know? She seemed to know what was happening before she lunged at me. But how?" Exhausted from tears and remorse, Dempster fell into a deep asleep.

The days of summer were much shorter now. It was once again time to prepare for the long winter ahead. Dempster built his nest higher with sticks and twigs to keep the snow from piling up inside and relined the cup with moss and birch bark to insulate his sleeping area. He began to save some food from every meal he ate and stash it nearby, especially under the overhang for easier access once the snows came.

Each day he would visit the places where Beatriss used to be, hoping it had been a very bad dream. He gazed up at the sky and watched Celeste and her family circle above preparing to migrate, his sadness quickly turned into bitterness. *You took the only friend I ever had.*

At times, he wondered if he would ever be the same.

Winter snows transformed the landscape. Only the strong and brave remained. Though the cold winds howled drifting newly fallen snow, it was peaceful on the mountain. Ironically, Dempster enjoyed the peace and tranquility. Very few animals ventured near his territory. Even flocks of chickadees would only pass through from time to time.

The air was fresh this sunny, cold winter day when Dempster awoke craving fresh meat. He knew exactly where to go as he flew toward a more level area of the mountain. A small herd of mule deer was making its way down the mountain to the valley below unaware of the predator stalking their endless trek.

Dempster stood motionless in a tall white pine tree watching the cougar race toward the unsuspecting herd, the soft powdery snow rising and falling like tiny crystals behind the advancing cat. Fatigued, the herd moved slowly. A young deer remained digging for grass buried beneath the snow. The doe never knew what hit her as the large cougar sunk his teeth deep into her throat killing her instantly, scattering the reminder of the herd.

With the lifeless body of the doe held firmly in the cougar's powerful jaw, it watched as the herd regrouped and quickly moved on. He dragged the small deer behind some large rocks and proceeded to enjoy his kill. Dempster sat patiently waiting his turn in awe of the huge cat's power and skill. Once the cougar had finished, Dempster had his feed of fresh meat.

He made many trips back and forth to his area burying raw meat in several places surrounding his nest. During the last excursion, he aborted his plan when he spotted something he had never seen before. With a piece of carrion sticking out either side of his beak he sat motionless in an evergreen watching the movement below. *These must be the humans Father warned us about* he surmised watching as the pair inspected his nest and the surrounding area.

"Wow, look at the size of that nest!" the young male said. "It must belong to an eagle or something."

The female was more interested in the flat snowy area that covered the pond. "Look at these pictures. I have never seen such abstract designs. It looks like whatever created them did so with its feet and beak. Whatever it is, it is quite the artist. They are fabulous."

The male took his place beside the female. "This is all too strange. What could have done this?"

"It has to be a bird of some type and it lives here permanently," she said gazing around the area. "I read that crows are the most intelligent birds in the world. So maybe it's a crow."

The male turned and looked at her. "Crows live in trees, not on mountains. Come on. It's going to get dark soon and we need to head back. This is far enough up the mountain."

Dempster had heard very little of their conversation, as the chickadees' loud warning sounded throughout the area. His thoughts went back to that horrible day, reliving the last few moments of his conversation with Beatriss, as he had many times. Only this time, he could hear the chickadees' loud cries warning them of impending danger as Celeste descended closer.

"Beatriss must have heard their warning." He thought back to that day on the rock when Beatriss wanted to move on because we were an easy target. *Instead I kept talking and put us both at risk. There is no doubt that she saved my life. I was the eagle's next meal.*

He gazed up toward the top of the mountain. "Beatriss saved my life." As tears stung his eyes he dropped the piece of carrion and flew over to his nest for the remainder of the day wondering if he would ever get over losing his only mentor.

Signs of spring finally began as the last traces of snow melted away. Animals came out of hibernation and flocks of birds returned to their nesting sites. Dempster looked up toward the top of Magassus feeling his heart beat faster as he watched Celeste riding the air currents. He was much more vigilant and cautious now. He knew his survival depended on it.

One morning after his bath, Dempster sat preening himself in a nearby tree when a couple of crows landed near the pond. The larger male began strutting around the area then turned to his mate. "This looks like a good location. It has everything we need to start a family, nest and all."

His mate wasn't as convinced. "It looks occupied," she said standing quietly near the pond observing the area.

Her partner took his place beside her. "I wonder if this is the home of the cackling crow of Magassus Mountain," she said. "Remember the story a member of the flock told us some time ago about a crow that wouldn't leave home so his family left without him."

He turned toward his mate. "Yeah, I remember. What a stupid crow. He could have had what we have," he cooed pecking her beak.

She pecked him back. "We certainly don't want to make our home here," she said taking flight with her partner close behind.

Chapter 8: The Pack

DEMPSTER REMAINED PERCHED in the tree long after the pair of crows had gone thinking about what they said. *Well at least I have a reputation. I bet not many crows have one,* he thought proudly puffing out his clean feathers.
Still, something stirred within him that he hadn't felt before when he saw the two crows together. *Am I really missing out on something* he wondered as this strange yearning took hold? He remembered how the pair spoke to one another; the love. They were definitely a dedicated couple.

That's it! I need a mate. I will get a mate and return to the mountain to live and raise a family like my parents did. He thought about them leaving him. *Only we will all stay here on Magassus forever.* Dempster felt better than he had in a long time.

The next few days Dempster made his way down Magassus and into a valley below searching for flocks of crows. It felt strange venturing to more flat, cultivated land. He was quite nervous. This was the first time he had left the mountain, and as a single crow he was vulnerable to all kinds of enemies.

He flew over farms with grain fields until he finally located an abandoned cornfield where many crows were pecking the ground for fallen seeds and insects. He landed on the barn's rusty old weather vane and sat mesmerized as crows of all sizes came and went. "Well, I guess there is no time like the present," he said, flying down to the field.

He made himself look handsome and confident, the way his father had shown him, and proceeded to strut over to a female crow pecking the damp ground for food. He was about to speak when another crow landed hard on his back causing him to lose his balance. "Hey, what's happening!" he yelled.

"What's happening? This is what's happening," the crow said, pecking hard at his head.

"What do you think you are doing?" Dempster said, finally wrestling the crow off his back.

"What do you think you are doing?" it retorted.

"I, I was just about to introduce myself," Dempster stammered, tidying his back feathers.

The other crow stood his ground and looked him in the eye. "To my intended mate?"

The cocky Dempster moved closer to him when he realized he was a head taller than his competition. "Your 'intended' mate? Obviously she hasn't given you an answer yet. And judging by the looks of you, I can understand why."

"Why you ..." the crow said, lunging at Dempster and knocking him back off his feet.

"Feisty little jerk!" Dempster said as he quickly regained his footing and lunged at his challenger. Feathers flew as the two crows fought each other with beaks and claws on the ground then in the air until one crow flew off. "And stay away," Dempster called after it.

He made himself look presentable as he strutted toward his prize who continued pecking the ground. Just like his Father before him he had won the fight to the finish. *She's all mine now. I'm the winner.*

"It looks like I've won myself a mate," Dempster said, standing tall in front of her with his rich black feathers puffed out.

She ignored him.

"Oh, playing hard to get are we?" Again, he thought of his parent's courtship. "Do you have any idea who I am? I am Dempster the crow, a.k.a. the star, firstborn of the great Armand and lovely Beth."

She turned and quickly flew to another part of the field.

"What the heck? Hey wait a minute," he said. He flew after her and landed nearby. "If you are playing hard to get I'm up for the challenge," he said, strutting confidently in front of her.

"I got this nest up on Magassus Mountain for us to go live in," he winked. "No doubt you will love it. What do you say?"

"What do I say?" she asked indignantly looking him straight in the eye. "I say you are the rudest crow I have ever seen. And even if you were the last crow on earth, I would not accompany you. I have never heard of anything so silly. You and me living on some stupid mountain together."

"Hey wait a minute," Dempster said defensively. "It's not a stupid mountain. It's my home. Like I said, you will love it. It kind of grows on you."

Again, there was no response from his intended. "Look, I just put my life on the line," *I really didn't. It was a done deal.* "And now I'm taking you with me to live on my mountain."

Their raised voices had attracted company as the surrounding crows moved closer. "What's this? A convention?" Dempster protested, looking around at the group that had gathered. "This is none of your business. Now get lost!"

"You get lost," an angry crow said, opening up a path through the crowd. It was the crow he had fought earlier.

Dempster looked at the surrounding mob. "I am Dempster the crow, a.k.a. the star, firstborn of the amazing Armand and the lovely ..."

"We know all about you," the crow interjected. "You live alone on Magassus Mountain because you are too into 'yourself' to live among other more civilized crows. And furthermore, you are not welcome here. Go back where you came from," the crow said firmly, as the female they had fought over joined him at his side.

Dempster could see he was outnumbered and had enough sense to realize he was no match for a pack of angry crows. "Your loss!" he yelled, before flying off.

Chapter 9: Alone Again, Naturally

HOME ON THE mountain never looked so good, Dempster thought strutting back and forth in front of his nest. "I don't need a mate. She is stupid. Not my mountain. She has no idea what an opportunity she gave up to stay with that weakling."

He breathed deeply and thought back to her saying he was the rudest crow she had ever seen. He had been on his own for so long that he lacked the skills necessary to socialize with others. But he would never admit it. "I don't need anybody. I like being alone on my mountain. It is all mine. This is where I'm staying forever," he vowed as a familiar emptiness took hold of him.

It was turning into a very hot, dry summer on Magassus. The pond was quickly drying up, as was the landscape. Dempster looked up at the cloudless sky. A relentless hot sun scorched the area he called home. He spent most of his time in the cool of the surrounding woods.

Animals of the mountain were on the move as lightning sparked forest fires in the higher elevations. Dempster watched from a nearby tree as a wolverine, the most vicious of all mountain mammals, made its way through the area, stopping to drink from the pond. The wolverine has no known natural enemies, and like the other animals in the area, Dempster didn't move a fraction until the wolverine moved on.

The next morning, Dempster woke up coughing and choking as thick grey smoke engulfed his area. "What the heck?" he sputtered trying to get his bearings. "I can't see. I can't breathe."

Violently choking and blinded by smoke, he managed to climb out of the nest. He moved cautiously keeping as close to the ground as possible to avoid the thicker smoke. He knew he had to leave but was unable to see any clear passage out. He began gulping in the acrid smoke as waves of panic got the better of him. Coughing and choking he tried to make his way to the edge of the cliff so he could fly off the mountain. He turned and stumbled. Losing his footing, he fell into a deep hole swallowing him as he lost consciousness.

Heavy rains began falling, gradually filling the hole with water. Dempster choked and sputtered as he regained consciousness. "Where am I? What's happening?" he yelled flailing in the muck.

He began to panic then remembered the dense smoke that covered this area of mountain. Looking up he could see the sky as the water began rising in the hole. "I'm alive!" he shouted, manoeuvring himself up and out of the hole onto muddy yet solid ground. He was shocked to see how far he had travelled from his nest and into this portion of the woods.

As the rain continued, Dempster watched as the hole that saved his life filled to the top with water and wondered how he had missed it during his exploration of the forest. The hole had been a lifesaver. If he hadn't fallen into it who knows what the outcome would have been.

He strutted throughout the familiar area he called home and breathed in the fresh clean air, as the rain continued to rejuvenate the mountain. "Yup, it takes more than some heavy smoke to take down `the star'," he yelled looking skyward.

Days of rain had returned life on the mountain back to normal. With the forest fires no longer a threat, Dempster was able to carry on his daily routine. Even the animals avoided his area once again.

One night he had just got settled in his nest when he saw tiny blinking lights circling just outside of it. "What in the world? Am I seeing things?" His curiosity got the better of him.

He jumped up onto the side of the nest for a closer look and found himself surrounded by many little flashing lights. *It must be some sort of insect* he surmised. "I could use a `light' snack," he chuckled. "Now there's a good one. A light snack because it lights up. Am I clever or what," he said, grabbing one out of the warm night air.

He no sooner swallowed the bug when he began retching. "Agggg!" he yelled in agony, as the next forceful retch sent him tumbling into the nest. He stumbled around the nest retching and retching like a mad crow. With one final retch, he threw up the nasty little creature. Exhausted, he fell asleep.

The next morning he examined the little culprit. It was one of those fireflies that his mother had warned them about. "I remember now. `If it blinks, think'," she had warned. "In other words think before you put it in your mouth."

The firefly produces steroids called lucibufagins that make birds ill. "Lesson learned. No more `light' snacks. I still think that is one of my better lines." He chuckled though not for long as his stomach still hurt from last night's retching.

A few nights later, he was in his nest ready to go to sleep when something glowing on the edge of it caught his eye. "What the heck?" His voice seemed to coax it closer. Dempster quickly jumped up on the opposite edge and watched as the glowing object jumped into his nest. "Well I never," he said, peering into it for a closer look. "Ahhh!" he yelled falling back over the edge as the object jumped up at him.

As the full moon came out from behind the clouds, Dempster watched a large toad with a glowing belly full of fireflies hop away. "Looks like they are the only creatures that can stomach a 'light' snack," he chuckled, remembering his own experience a few nights before.

"Hopefully there won't be any more disruptions. I need my beauty sleep," he yawned climbing back into the nest.

The days began shortening and the leaves were turning bright red and gold. Dempster watched as long lines of migrating birds marked the fall skies with flocks heading south for the winter. He glanced around his area where he'd be spending another winter.

"Well, at least it will be more peaceful and quiet. Hey! Get lost!" he shouted as a chipmunk ran from the pond. "Soon they will be hibernating too. Then I will be on my own. The way I like it. No one around. I like it here on my mountain." He stood quietly looking skyward until his neck started to ache.

Like the past summer on Magassus, winter proved to be as challenging. Biting, gusty winds, and heavy snows battered the mountain slope. Dempster was forcded to seek refuge in the woven branches of cedar trees, as often his nest was buried by deep snow. There were many hungry days spent perched in the middle of the cedars deep in the forest, preserving his energy. The heavy snows kept other mountain animals close to shelter.

Whenever conditions were favourable, Dempster had to scout further for signs of winter kill that had been left by the mountain's fierce hunters. Thankfully, it was easy to locate any fresh blood stains splashed wildly on the white landscape. He would spend hunger driven hours discovering where the kill had taken place and be justly rewarded for his time. He would sit patiently waiting for the stalker to semi-bury the lifeless carcass then fly in for a meal stuffing himself with frozen flesh.

A few days later, Dempster watched a herd of mountain goats make their way up and down the rocky crags and steep slopes in perfect ease. The herd walked calmly along narrow ledges overlooking a deep snow filled canyon. To a crow, it seemed like one wrong step and they would plummet to their death.

Little did he know that mountain goats have hooves especially designed for mountain climbing. In the center of its divided hoof there is a spongy pad that enables the animal to cling to narrow ledges or rocky hillsides without slipping. As they made their way down the cliff, there was always a cougar waiting on flat land to take down the sick or young. Dempster found that the thrill of watching the cougar take down the animal was almost as good as the fresh meat it left behind after a feed. He would fill his stomach then begin the relentless task of transporting meat back to his nesting area.

After what seemed to be endless weeks of cold and snow the daylight hours began increasing. The deep snow started receding throughout his area and Dempster could finally sleep in his nest and take a bath along the edges of the pond. The air was fresh though chilly but the sun shone brightly. He watched as flocks of birds returned to their nesting grounds and hibernating animals were once again a challenge for him to keep at bay.

Though he no longer searched the places where Beatriss used to be, he still wished she was here on Magassus, not too close of course, but nearby. He would often think of the family that deserted him and the bitterness inside would consume him. *It was not supposed to be like this. How could they just leave me like they did? I will never forgive them.*

It was early spring and life on the mountain was alive with new growth and of course new animal life. One night Dempster was just dozing off when loud mysterious calls of short, high-pitched notes, repeated 100 to 130 times per minute, permeated the surrounding woods.

"What the heck? How am I supposed to get my much needed sleep with all this racket?"

"Quiet!" he yelled in vain as the incessant whistling continued. It was just before sun up when the noise finally stopped allowing him to get some sleep.

The next morning, Dempster felt as if his head was full of dead moss from lack of sleep and vowed to get to the bottom of this deafening noise. After filling his stomach, he searched the nearby trees but didn't find the source. "Well, hopefully whatever it was has gone now."

But that night, the noise started up again. Dempster hopped up onto the side of his nest and instead of yelling out, he calmly scoured the trees letting his ears guide his eyes to the source. There on the bottom branch of a small evergreen sat a miniature owl. On another branch close by two more sat.

After closer inspection in the full moon's light he decided they were saw-whet owls, the only owls that aren't a threat to crows. He watched as one swooped down and picked up a deer mouse running across the area.

"Hey! What do you think you are doing?" Dempster questioned as he watched the tiny specimen return to the lower branch of a conifer.

There was no reply.

"Get lost!" he yelled.

The whistling chorus started up. The moon kept going in and out of the clouds so it was difficult to see them. Frustrated he yelled over the deafening noise, "I will deal with you tomorrow morning." In his nest, he folded his wings over his head to drown out the incessant whistling that continued throughout most of the night.

During his search the next morning, it seemed they vanished in thin air. "And stay away," he yelled for good measure.

That night as he lay in his nest enjoying the peace and quiet, he realized that was how a male saw-whet owl attracted a mate. Just like crows, they had their own rituals. His thoughts turned to the female crow he had fought for and lost. He fell asleep dreaming of how life would have been if she had accompanied him back to the mountain.

The days were long and warm. The area he called home was relatively quiet now, especially at night, as partnerships turned into families. Dempster often thought of what his offspring would be like. The males would be handsome, intelligent, brave, confident, artistic, witty, and humorous, like their father. The females would be beautiful, patient, and kind like their mother.

He had no idea what had come over him lately thinking about all this mate and family stuff. "Ah, who needs it," he said, pulling leaves off a fleabane plant to line his nest. The tics, mites, and lice in the nest were driving him crazy and lining his nest with these leaves would exude potent chemicals that inhibit parasite growth.

When he finished lining the nest, he walked around looking for a large anthill. After a short search, he located one and sprawled across it. Covering the nest with his body provoked the insects, causing them to run in and out of his feathers. The agitated ants released formic acid, a natural insecticide that kills the parasites. While he waited for the ants to perform their magic, he scooped up some ants in his bill, crushing them to release the acid, and then proceeded to smear the corpses over his body.

"That's much better," he said, standing up and shaking off the remaining ants.

He stood silently observing the area. "Beatriss was right." `*If you disturb their nest, they just move to another location*'. The anthill was over by her favourite rock last year.

Thinking about Beatriss, he looked up and saw Celeste circling the heavens. He assumed, or rather he hoped, that the eagle had other food sources and wasn't interested in crow meat. To be safe, he remained much more vigilant during the summer months as he flew into the woods for a meal.

After a slug meal he flew back to his area and sat in a nearby tree preening himself before heading back to the nest for a nap. He was about to fly to his nest when an intruder drinking at his pond caught his eye. Dempster watched closely as the nosy individual examined his nest before returning to the pond for another drink of water. This unwelcome guest seemed to have no intention of leaving.

"Well, well, well. It looks like I have company," he said quietly taking wing.

Dempster landed silently behind his victim, who was drinking quietly, unaware of his presence. "What are you doing on my mountain?" he bellowed.

Book Two

Addy

Addy, content to remain with her family is devastated when they leave her to fend for herself. Driven by her fear of being alone to face the world, she makes a dangerous trek to convince the crow residing on Magassus to change the 'Law of Nature' so all offspring can remain with their parents.

Chapter 1: The Brood

SPRING WAS LATE arriving in Blackburn County. Though the last traces of snow were gone, there was a nip in the air that even the mid-May sun couldn't warm.

"I do hope it warms up soon," Mother said, as she sank down lower into the cup of her nest incubating four eggs.

Father robin, on a branch nearby, nodded thinking back to the adverse conditions he had encountered while scouting around for their new home. On the day of his arrival, the sun was shining brightly offering renewed hope of an early warm spring. The next day, a late spring blizzard all but obliterated the landscape. He had managed to seek shelter in the woven branches of an old cedar tree to wait out the storm. The next morning, a thick blanket of snow covered the forest, but a relentless sun had returned, filling him with new hope that spring was just around the corner.

Today, as he sat on the branch just above his mate, his song was filled with pride, for soon he would be a father.

"I am hungry. I will grab something to eat then be right back," Mother said, not wanting to be too far from the nest.

Father hopped down to the nest and gazed in at the bluish green eggs. One of the eggs seemed to be moving. He stuck his head down for a closer look.

"It is moving!" he said. "Mother, come quick!" Just as she flew up to the nest, the first of their creations was emerging. Father could hardly control his excitement as the helpless creature lay sprawled over the remaining eggs and broken eggshell.

"I have a son!" Father cried. "His name will be J.D."

As Mother went to sit back down on the remaining eggs, two more started hatching.

"It's a girl!" Mother squealed. "Judith will be her name."

The third egg produced another son.

"Welcome to the world Andrew," Father said, as he dropped pieces of broken eggshell over the edge of the nest. "I am so happy. Two sons and one daughter. What more could parents ask for?"

"Another daughter or son," Mother replied. Father had forgotten the fourth egg in his excitement. Both parents watched for any life emerging from the remaining egg.

"It won't be long now. Not all babies hatch at the same time," she explained.

It wasn't until the next morning, after sunrise, that Addy pecked her way out of her shell (with a little help from her mother). Now their family was complete. The parents spent the first several days keeping the nestlings warm and well nourished, while keeping a vigilant eye out for enemies with an appetite for newborns. It was a very exhausting time for both parents, especially for Father. He made a hundred trips or more each day searching for spiders, grasshoppers, crickets, June bugs, earthworms, clover leaves, and grasses to feed the brood.

By the seventh day, four pairs of eyes would watch for them. The days had finally warmed up, enabling their parents to be away from the nest for longer periods of time.

They were a handsome brood. As their feathers began to grow, their own distinct personalities developed also. J.D. was the largest of the four and was way ahead of his time. Judith was the most dignified of the group. She always held her head high. Andrew was full of mischief and was forever teasing the girls, especially Addy. Timid Addy was content just being with all her family.

As Mother or Father approached the nest, they would chirp loudly with mouths wide open for the food. J.D. always managed to get the most, probably because he was the oldest and most aggressive. Judith was well mannered and would patiently wait her turn. Andrew was another story. He would walk over the girls in his quest to be second in line. Addy needed special attention, as she would not assert herself in any way. Mother seemed especially more aware of Addy's diffident nature and would often feed her first.

"I am worried about Addy," Mother confided to Father as they searched for worms together. "She is not like the other three. They are anxious to fly, leave the nest and take care of themselves. But Addy is very clingy."

"She will come around," Father concluded. "Being the last born, she is immature, the baby of the family. I am sure she will follow J.D.'s example and come into her own also. You worry too much." Somehow, Mother was not as positive.

On the tenth day, an eerie silence engulfed the area. No other birds were flying about or chirping. Everyone seemed frozen in their area. Mother and Father were both at the nest and under no circumstances were any of the brood to make a peep. Addy was most frightened. Her mother knew this and stayed by her side. This strange silence was finally broken by a piercing scream from the grackle nest in a neighbouring spruce tree sending every bird within earshot into a frenzied mass crying out warnings. But it was too late. In one foul swoop, the largest bird the brood had ever seen grabbed one of the grackle babies and flew to another tree and proceeded to tear it apart and eat it.

"Father, what is it?" J.D. asked.

"It is a crow. Every bird's deadliest enemy. For it will stop at nothing when it comes to filling its face. The crows know the location of every nest long before the eggs are in it. They stalk the area while the nests are being constructed."

The mother grackle was beside herself with grief. Her frustrated screams brought other grackles to the area who tried in vain to save her baby. They took turns swooping at the crow that was enjoying his fresh meal undeterred by their continual cries and attacks. Every bird within earshot had arrived. It is the only time all birds unite, no matter what the species.

When the huge crow finished his meal, he let out loud caws of satisfaction that drowned out the distress cries of the other birds. He dropped the remainder of the carcass then flew off with some grackles in pursuit.

The robins sat quietly and watched as a steady flow of grackles landed in the tree offering their condolences to the bereaved parents.

"Please pay close attention to what I have to say," Father began. "I am sorry you had to witness that attack by the crow. But that was an example of one of the many enemies you may encounter throughout your lives."

"What are enemies?" J.D. asked, as he vibrated his wings.

"Anyone who will harm you. This could be animals, other birds, or people."

"What's people?" Andrew asked, as he shoved Addy to the side of the nest.

"I don't know," Mother replied. "Your father has seen people before. I know you have to fly into the valley to see them. Some robins even make their homes near where people live."

"People are not like us at all," Father said. "They walk on two legs like us, but they don't have wings so they can't fly. Instead, they have two arms with hands on each end. When I was a youngster, I saw a person pull our neighbour's nest apart with their hands and take the babies away. The parents never saw their brood again. It is best not to build a nest near people."

"Animals like raccoons, opossums, squirrels, and snakes like to eat our eggs," Father continued. "Crows, blue jays, and hawks like our eggs also. They also feed on young, helpless babies, as you witnessed today, to satisfy their carnivorous appetites. Unfortunately, we have many enemies, so we must be forever vigilant in our quest to survive."

"Being helpful and kind is also important, as you may need somebody's assistance one day," Mother added.

"Aw, I'm not afraid of anything," Andrew said.

"Be wary my son. Always expect the unexpected," Mother warned.

"It is time for all of you to have a nap. This has been a very traumatic experience," Mother said, before flying off for a meal.

While her brothers and sister slept, Addy remained wide awake. Fear had consumed every part of her. *I don't ever want to be by myself. I am never leaving this nest. I will stay here safe and sound with my mother and father forever. My parents will take care of me.* Content with this thought, Addy fell fast asleep.

Chapter 2: On My Own

ON THE FOURTEENTH day, Mother and Father remained on the ground.

"Youngsters," Father called up to the brood. "It's time to fly down here and get your own breakfast."

The four of them looked down at their parents standing below. J.D. was the first to fly out of the nest. This was really no surprise, as he had been exercising his wings on the edge of the nest for days just waiting for this moment. With one powerful thrust, he was soaring over to the furthest tree. Addy watched him in awe. She was so proud of him. She thought J.D. must mean 'just dandy' because that is what he was.

"Come on," he yelled, waving to the others to join him. "This is fun."

Andrew was next to fly. He didn't go as far as J.D. "One day I will go further than you J.D.," he called out.

Judith hopped up onto the edge of the nest. With one graceful swoop, she flew to a neighbouring tree not too far from the nest. She would never compete with her brothers.

Addy looked down from the nest. Her brothers and sister had joined their parents on the ground and were competing for the worms they were pulling up.

"I'm up here," Addy called out. No one was listening. They were making such a racket competing for the worms there was no way they could hear her.

"Mother, Father," she cried out. "Don't forget me."

Addy watched in disbelief as they continued to ignore her. By the time her mother flew up to the nest she was frantic and starving. Her mother had brought her a big earthworm which Addy devoured quickly.

"Mother, I thought you had forgotten me. I called and called but nobody heard me."

"You can't stay in the nest. You must fly down and join your brothers and sister. You are old enough to learn how to feed yourself."

"Mother, you can feed me. I will learn how to fly so I can stay with you all the time."

Her mother put her wing around her. "Addy, it's time for you to make a life of your own like your siblings. In a few months, you will be fully grown and ready to start a family of your own."

"But Mother, I don't want to leave you and Father."

"You must Addy. Father and I are preparing to start another brood very soon. We have given you life, now you must begin to live it."

As Addy watched her mother fly back down to the rest of the family, she started to cry.

"Cry baby. Cry baby."

Addy looked up to where the voice was coming from and there sat a blue jay on the branch above. She was in such a state from crying, she couldn't send out a warning to the others.

"Why are you crying? Are you a big baby?" he chided.

"I, I don't want to leave my parents," Addy sputtered.

"You have to leave your parents. All offspring must leave their parents. It is the 'law of nature'. Just ask the cackling crow of Magassus Mountain." With that, the blue jay flew off.

Her mother returned to the nest with another worm. Addy gobbled it down trying to speak while she ate.

"You will choke if you talk while eating," Mother cautioned.

Addy swallowed it down. "Mother, Mother! The biggest blue jay landed on that branch," she said pointing up at it, "and he didn't eat me! I was crying so I couldn't send out a warning to you and the others. He spoke to me. Why didn't he eat me?"

A concerned look came over her mother's face as she glanced around the tree to make sure the blue jay was gone.

"You are probably too large for him to eat. Either that or he just wasn't hungry. Addy, you must never let your guard down. He is one of our enemies and could have attacked you."

"Could it be not all blue jays are enemies? He was trying to help me."

"Help you?" What did he say?"

"I told him I didn't want to leave you and Father and he said I have no choice. It is the 'law of nature'. Do I have to leave you and Father?"

Mother sighed. "In this instance, the blue jay is right. You, your brothers and sister must get on with your lives. The sooner you leave this nest the better."

"Mother, don't leave me," Addy called out, as she watched her fly out of sight.

J.D. flew up to the nest. "Come on Addy. How come you are still sitting up here? There is a big, beautiful world out there just waiting for you to explore."

"J.D. I'm frightened."

"Frightened? Of what?"

"Of being on my own away from Mother and Father," she said with tears welling up in her eyes.

"Awe, come on Addy. Unless you at least try to make a go of it on your own, you will never know if you can."

"Aren't you afraid to leave home?"

"Heck no. I could hardly wait to be old enough to be on my own. I have already met up with others my age and I am having a great time. I won't be returning to the nest. I've got a life. But I will watch for you, Addy. Come on now, get on with it. Good luck. Good-bye Addy."

Addy watched J.D. fly off into the woods wishing she could be more like him. She was sure he was kidding. *He will be back.*

As the last traces of daylight faded, Addy could hear a robin's song in the distance confirming the day was coming to an end. *Where is my family?* She watched for their return until it was too dark to see. Finally, she realized they were not coming home. Hungry and tired, she sank down deep into the nest and cried herself to sleep.

Marking the dawn of a new day, a robin greeted it with its song somewhere in the distance. Addy opened her eyes and in dawn's early light was able to see she was alone in the nest. The surrounding branches near the nest were unoccupied also. Addy called out for her mother and father. When they did not respond to her cries, she started to panic. Crying and calling for them, she jumped up onto the edge of the nest. As she looked down to the ground below where they usually ate, she lost her footing and began to fall. Instinctively, she flapped her wings as hard as she could and landed safely on the ground. Her heart was pounding so hard, she was sure her chest would split open releasing it. She looked all around her. The ground was a lot different from being up in a tree. Creatures of all shapes and sizes were busy going about their business. *I must keep alert, for who knows what enemies are lurking about.*

Hunger pangs were overriding her fear. *But how do I feed myself?* She wished she had paid more attention to the family lesson on feeding instead of crying in the nest. She hopped over to a patch of clover and started to pull at the tender plants. A spider in the middle of the patch was her first catch. As she pulled at the plants, another robin landed close by. Addy hopped over to where he was feeding, only to realize that it wasn't J.D., Andrew or Judith as she had hoped.

"What are you staring at? Didn't your mother teach you it is not polite to stare? One would think you are quite nosy."

"I am sorry. I thought you were one of my siblings. I was just watching you fetch worms," she replied.

"Didn't your mother teach you anything?" he asked, rolling his eyes skyward.

"I just left the nest this morning. Up until now, my mother and father were feeding me."

"How old are you?" he asked in an authoritative voice.

"Seventeen days, I believe."

"I left the nest when I was way younger than that," he chuckled.

"How old are you?"

"Thirteen days old," he chirped proudly. "How come it took you so long?" he asked sarcastically.

"I didn't want to leave my mother and father. As it turned out, they left me." Addy could feel a lump in her throat as she tried to be brave and keep from crying. "But they will be back for me. I know they will."

"Oh grow up. Every robin must leave its parents." With that he pulled up another worm and swallowed it down.

"You must know all about the 'law of nature'," she concluded.

He just gave her a funny look before flying off.

He is either very rude or he is not as smart as he thinks he is. Again, hunger surpassed her loneliness. She had watched him pull enough worms out of the ground to try it herself. After a few tries, she pulled out a fat juicy earthworm and swallowed it down, then another. Finally, her tummy was full. She felt so proud knowing she could get her own meals now. But even a full stomach couldn't take her mind off being on her own. Addy looked up into the trees.

"Mother, Father, I am down here. Please come and get me. I am so lonely and afraid. Where are you?" she called out.

Her cries had not gone unheard. Cardinals, chickadees, sparrows, and grackles were in the trees surrounding her and hopping about on the ground.

"Cry baby, cry baby," the cardinals chanted forming a circle around her. The other birds soon joined in the chorus.

"Ba bee beebeebeebee," the chickadees sang.

Addy quickly realized they were not here on a social visit. She put her wings over her ears to muffle their name calling hoping they would go away. Instead the chanting persisted. They were not leaving. Addy ran forward a few steps and in one quick motion, she flew up and away to another part of the forest. Panting from the fear she felt and her first major flight, she landed in a large maple tree and hid behind a large green leaf. She closed her eyes for a moment and when she opened them again, the sun was shining on her. She must have fallen asleep.

Chapter 3: Delvin

ADDY AWOKE SUDDENLY when the branch she was perched on jerked forward with a gust of warm air. Her eyes widened as she looked around. "Where am I? Now I am really lost. I have got to find my mother and father," she cried out.

"Why? You are big enough to look after yourself."

Addy looked up to where the voice was coming from and froze. On a larger branch just above her and over to the right was perched a hawk finishing off the remnants of a quail. The hawk released the remainder of the carcass and flew down beside her.

"Please don't eat me!" she wailed crouching down as close to the branch as possible.

The hawk chuckled to himself. "I have just eaten," he replied looking down at his last meal. "A little too boney for my liking."

Addy was so petrified she had dug her nails so far into the branch that she could not fly away even if she had wanted to. Here was one of the enemies her father had warned her about sitting so close she could see the blood of his last victim coated around his beak. She wanted her mother and father desperately because she did not have any idea what to do. Her instincts were telling her to send out a warning cry but when she tried, only a little squeak came out.

"Please don't be afraid of me. I am not going to hurt you," he said calmly.

She was too young and naive to believe otherwise.

"What is your name?" the hawk queried. Aware of her overwhelming fear, he introduced himself.

My name is Delvin," he said, nodding his head.

"Adddddddy," she replied sounding more like a telegraph machine than a robin. Delvin furrowed his brow. "Adddddddy," he repeated.

She took a deep breath. "Addy."

"Addy," he nodded. "That is a nice name. I like that."

As their eyes met for a brief moment, she couldn't help but notice the kindness that was there. Still, she began to shake uncontrollable.

"Please, don't be afraid of me," Delvin coaxed, as he watched her tremble. "You have my word. I mean you no harm."

Even though Addy knew it was wrong to accuse someone of something unless you were sure, her fear overruled. She took a deep breath to calm herself. "I am not trying to be rude, but you are my enemy," she said, feeling a tad braver. "I am probably your next meal and I want you to know that I am not afraid."

"How courageous of you," Delvin chuckled. "But like I said before, I have no intentions of making a meal out of you. I make it a point of not getting to know my next prey on a first name basis."

"You don't?" she replied, feeling somewhat relieved.

"Well, not today anyway," he laughed.

Again, fear covered her face.

"Lighten up Addy. I was joshing you. The truth is, I would like to be your friend."

Now she was really confused. "I don't understand. How can you be a friend to me when every robin knows hawks are our enemies?"

"Well, not all enemies are foes. Quite often, we share the same thoughts and feelings. I, as you, need love, understanding and friendship. Sometimes in our quest to satisfy these needs, we reach out to those who are just as vulnerable as ourselves. These needs can override our specie differences making the most unlikely friendships quite compatible. Addy, we are all wonderful creatures of this beautiful earth. And all creatures, no matter what the specie, need to feel connected. Sometimes these connections happen when we least expect them."

She could not quite comprehend what he had just said. However, they did have one thing in common. They were both all alone. But still, all that her parents had taught her was being totally contradicted by this hawk. She still wasn't sure whether to believe him. Suddenly, a sick feeling came over her. *Maybe he is trying to trick me into thinking he is my friend when really all I am is an easy meal. He is standing so close to me he could tear my head off without leaving the branch* she thought lowering her head into her shoulders.

Surprisingly, in one quick swoop, Delvin flew off the branch. The wind from his wings ruffled her feathers, as she watched him disappear into the woods.

"He's gone!" she breathed deeply. *Maybe he was telling the truth after all. But friends with a hawk? Too unbelievable.* It was imperative that she find her mother and father, as she was very confused.

Chapter 4: The Law of Nature

ADDY COULD TELL by the position of the sun that it was getting close to supper. *I will eat with my parents* she thought and proceeded to fly back home. Her sense of direction was very accurate, for on the first try, she managed to locate the nest with her mother sitting on it.

"Mother, you are back! I knew you wouldn't desert me," she cried, landing on the same branch.

Her mother looked surprised to see her, sinking down deeper into the cup.

"Why are you sitting on our nest again?"

"Your father and I have started another brood."

"That is great! More brothers and sisters. I can help you feed and look after them. Oh Mother, isn't that wonderful?"

Her mother took a deep breath and shook her head. "For the last time Addy, you must leave home and make a life of your own like your sister and brothers. You cannot stay here any longer. Your father and I will love you forever but you must go and not come back," her mother said firmly.

Addy felt her heart sink. The pain she felt was unbearable. "But Mother..."

"Go!" her mother cried.

She looked at her mother in shock and disbelief for she had never spoken to her like this before. Pain mixed with pride forced Addy to fly off. It was almost dark when she landed in a towering oak tree. Confused and tired from flying, she closed her eyes to block out this horrible world.

Just before the first light of dawn, a robin's song broke the early morning silence. More alone than ever, Addy felt tears stinging her eyes once again. "What will I do now? Where will I go? Who will take care of me? I am so afraid."

"You are a brave girl, Addy."

"Delvin!" she exclaimed in a relieved yet guarded voice. There he was in all his glory watching her from a nearby branch. Suddenly, nothing mattered to her. If Delvin wanted to eat her, so be it. She didn't care anymore. "I am too weary to put up a fight Delvin. I am only 19 days old and I feel like I have already lived a lifetime. If you want to eat me, breakfast is ready."

Delvin shook his head. "Addy, all I want is your friendship."

Addy stared at him in disbelief. "So be it," she sighed. "You are all I have. Imagine being friends with a hawk. No one would ever believe it. Then again, who can I tell? Who cares?"

Delvin landed close to her. "You had better get something to eat. You missed your supper last night and I am sure your long flight has left you hungry."

How did he know all that? Still, he was right. She was starving.

After she had eaten, she flew back up to the branch. Delvin had sat quietly waiting for her. She turned to look at him. There was a calmness about him. He had sharp eyes that wouldn't miss a thing, yet they were kind and receptive to her. He was a handsome bird, much larger than herself, with reddish brown markings on his underside. He always held his head high, to a height that demanded respect for all he encountered. As she sat admiring his incredible self-confidence, she could feel herself losing control again, as both fear and sadness welled up in her. She looked straight ahead so he wouldn't see the tears in her eyes.

"What is it Addy?"

"Oh Delvin, what will I do? My mother and father don't want me anymore. My mother sent me away last night for good. I can never go home again. I can't understand how any mother could send her offspring away. I would never do that to any of my brood. All I want to do is stay with them forever."

Delvin sat patiently listening while she unloaded all her pain and sadness. "Addy, your mother loves you very much. She told you so last night. But, she is correct in sending you away. You must make a life of your own now. One day, you will be a mother yourself and you must send your offspring on their way to live out their lives as mothers and fathers. That is how your species is reproduced, guaranteeing future generations of robins."

"You must know all about the 'law of nature', she replied.

"The 'law of nature'? I have never heard of it. What is it?"

"I don't know. When I was very young, I didn't want to leave the nest, so I started to cry. A blue jay that was nearby made fun of me and told me I had to because it was the 'law of nature'."

"Those blue jays are a cocky bunch that always have something to say," Delvin replied, trying to console her.

"Who made up this law?" he asked skeptically.

"I am not sure. The blue jay told me there is a crow on Magassus Mountain who knows all about it. But I am not sure who the crow is or for that matter, where Magassus Mountain is."

Delvin shifted a little on the branch. He had heard stories about a crow living all alone over on Magassus but never gave it any thought.

Addy turned to look at him. "I've got it!" I am going to go to the mountain and find this crow and convince him to change the law so that all offspring can stay with their parents if they want to."

A worried look came over Delvin's face. "Addy, you can't travel over to the mountain. You are far too young and it is very dangerous. Even I would never venture that far." He could see the look of determination on her face and it frightened him. "Addy, this is nonsense. Please reconsider. I could never accompany you on this journey for I am a woodland hawk. My home is here in the forest, as yours is. I can take care of you here. I will be there for you when others turn you away. Now that your mother and father have started another brood, you will need a friend more than ever."

Addy turned sharply toward Delvin. The only way he would have known about the new family was by following her. *He must have witnessed that horrible moment when Mother sent me away.* She felt a tug in her heart as she thought about his dedication to her. *Maybe he is a genuine friend and really does want to take care of me* she sighed. *But I don't belong with him. My place is with my parents.*

"Delvin, you are probably the only bird on the face of this earth that cares about me. For that I am truly grateful. But we come from different backgrounds. Your specie is an enemy to mine. We are a quick meal in a pinch. This friendship can go no further because I must venture to the mountain, find the crow and get him to change the 'law of nature' so I can live with my parents."

He was devastated by her decision. Even though he had only known her a short time, they shared a mutual bond.

"Addy, please don't go. It is too dangerous and there are so many things that can happen and I won't be there to help you. Besides, everything you need to survive is right here in the forest; food, shelter, other robins. I don't want you to go. I care."

"Then you will have to eat me."

"Don't be silly. You know I would never do that. You mean too much to me. Please reconsider."

Addy took a deep breath. "Delvin, do you know where Magassus Mountain is?"

He hesitated then answered. "Yes, I do."

"Good. We can spend the rest of the day together making our way through the woods so you can point me in the right direction. At first light of day tomorrow, I will be leaving for Magassus."

Delvin had seen the mountain from a tall balsam where he often went to think. He knew they were almost at the edge of the forest and gave some thought of taking her back deeper into the woods, but he knew this was selfish. She was determined to make the journey, with or without his help.

He swallowed hard trying to make the most out of a hopeless situation. "I would be proud to escort you to the edge of the woods, for I have seen the mountain from the tallest balsam."

"Thank you Delvin," she said, somewhat leery of her decision. They spent the remainder of the day making their way to the forest edge.

"Follow me," Delvin said, as he took flight for the final time.

As they approached a patch of balsam firs, one stood noticeably higher than the others. He landed close to the top branch of it with Addy close behind.

"What a magnificent tree," she cried.

"This is one of my favourite places. I can view the woods and land between here and Magassus."

Addy caught her breath almost falling off the branch as she viewed the mountain."Oh my!" she exclaimed feeling both elated and overwhelmed at the same time. "It is absolutely beautiful," she said trembling. Luckily the wind had picked up so Delvin couldn't tell it was her shaking the branch.

Rising up to greet a crimson sky, Magassus Mountain stood alone. Its highest peak surrounded by a thick halo of purple-grey clouds shaded red by the setting sun. Green waves of plush vegetation covered the leeward side.

As Addy observed Magassus, she began to have second thoughts. *Where is my head at? Maybe Delvin is right and I shouldn't go.* 'Do not be afraid', a voice inside her was saying. 'You have got to find out about the "law of nature" and not settle until it is changed'.

"Are you sure you want to go through with this?" Delvin asked.

Addy drew a deep breath. "Yes. More than ever."

"You had better get something to eat. It is starting to get dark," Delvin said, before flying off to get his own meal. He knew how upsetting it was for her to watch him eat the game he caught.

Addy ate and then settled in for the night on a smaller balsam. She could see the mountain from where she was perched and again contemplated tomorrow's journey. *It is not that far away. I will be back in no time.*

Delvin lighted on the branch beside her. They sat in silence as darkness descended.

"The mountain is not too far away. It won't take me long. I will be back before you know it," she said confidently.

He knew it was further away than Addy realized for distance could be deceptive. He also knew of the dangers involved on such a long journey. Outside the encompassing arms of the forest was a whole other world. One even he would not venture into. He made one last attempt to talk her out of it, but her mind was made up. She was leaving for the mountain at daybreak.

The first song of a robin awoke Addy with a start, for this was the day. She turned to her left and there was Delvin wide awake. He had spent a fitful night sleeping then waking. He was already sick with worry.

"You had better get a good breakfast in you, Addy." On that note, he flew off. She wondered if he would be back to see her off. Even the first dull light of dawn couldn't hide the glistening of tears in the corners of his eyes. *Be strong* she told herself. *I must do this.*

With her stomach full, she headed to the top branch of the lookout balsam. The morning had dawned sunny and warm. Addy glanced around once more before releasing herself from the safety of the forest. She looked down and there was Delvin perched just below her. "That's a switch. You are usually above me," she said, trying to make light of the situation.

"Addy, please be careful. I will be waiting here for you when you get back."

"Thank you, Delvin. I was hoping you would be. You are such a good friend. Thanks for believing in me. I must do this. After all, what good are wings if we never learn to fly?"

Addy let go of the branch and flew straight up. Her journey had begun.

Delvin had never felt so helpless and alone.

Chapter 5: My Friend

DELVIN WATCHED AS Addy disappeared from sight. He did not move until she was just a speck on the vast horizon.

"Please take care of yourself, Addy."

He turned himself around on the branch and saw a quail running through the woods until it ran out of sight. He never left the tree. Hours passed and he remained stationary. He had lost his only friend and with it went his appetite. He just didn't care. Nothing seemed to matter anymore, as once again he was on his own.

Why did he let her go? But he hadn't. Addy was determined to make the trek. Nothing he could have said or done would have changed her mind. She was more independent than she gave herself credit for. He was very proud of her. In fact, she had come such a long way on her own that he couldn't understand why she wanted to change the 'law'. *I guess she is just headstrong* he thought shaking his head.

Addy had rapidly matured physically in the last few days. He hoped it was enough to see her through her journey. But what if it wasn't? Again, worry consumed him.

Delvin turned to face Magassus. The sun seemed to be resting on its highest peak. In less than an hour, it will have consumed it for another day. He sat gazing at the mountain. Suddenly, it didn't seem so far away.

Chapter 6: The Trek

ADDY'S FIRST DAY of flight went without incident. She was tired and hungry having only stopped twice in one of the vast forest areas that covered the route to Magassus. She could see the sun setting behind the mountain and knew it was time to call it a day. It was paramount that her strength match her determination.

Landing in a cluster of trees, she chose one that faced Magassus. *I must never lose sight of the mountain. My whole future depends on it. I will be back home with my parents soon.*

Almost too tired to eat, she swooped down below and quickly filled her stomach with insects and worms and then returned to the branch. *I am almost there* or so she thought. Her eyes grew heavy, for it had been a very tiring day both physically and mentally. With the image of the mountain planted firmly in her mind, she was asleep before the last song of the robin.

At the break of dawn Addy awoke. Stretching and getting her bearings, she looked toward Magassus.

"It's gone!" she yelled almost falling off the tree branch. "Where is the mountain?"

Thinking she must have turned on the branch during the night, she made a full turn. Still, there was no mountain.

"Oh what will I do? Where will I go? I am lost," she cried as panic set in.

"How dare you interrupt my sleep?"

Addy froze in fear. She had never heard such a gruff voice in her life.

"Whooooo do you think you are you little wimp, disturbing me with all that silly racket?"

Addy swallowed hard and looked toward the voice. Less than two metres away perched a large great horned owl.

Another enemy. Stay calm and polite. "I am sorry. It's just that I am on my way to Magassus Mountain and I seem to have lost sight of it."

The owl chuckled to himself. *Another feather brain.* Tired as he was, he thought *I will have a little fun with this one.*

"I made the mountain disappear."

Addy's eyes widened. "You did?"

"Of course, us great horned owls are magic. Now that he had her undivided attention it was time to show off. "Want to see another magic trick? Look down at my right foot and watch my outer toe."

Addy watched in awe as the owl directed it forward, outward and completely backward. Then he got the toe on his left foot going.

"Oh my goodness, you really are magic." She had never seen anything as clever in her life.

As the sun drew higher in the sky, the owl could see the outline of Magassus becoming clearer. Addy had not taken her eyes off his toes.

"Listen kid, go and get yourself some breakfast and by the time you get back to your branch, I will have the mountain back."

"Are you that clever?"

"You bet."

By the time Addy flew back up to the branch, the mountain was in clear view.

"You did it!" she exclaimed. "But how?"

"Pure magic," he replied. "After all, I am a GREAT horned owl. Talented too. Say, why is the mountain so important to a little whippersnapper like you?"

"I am going there to get the cackling crow that lives on the mountain to change the 'law of nature'."

"The 'law of nature'?" *Now there's a new one. That line may come in handy some day* he thought making a mental note.

Addy proceeded to explain the law to him. The owl yawned, growing too tired to listen. After all, he had just gotten home.

He looked at the young robin. "Get going before I make you disappear. I need my beauty sleep. You don't get this handsome and great on two hours sleep, now be off with you," he said, flicking his wing skyward.

Addy did not delay. She managed to thank him for returning the mountain before she flew away.

"Poor kid. I hope she makes it." He didn't give her a second thought before he fell asleep.

As Addy took off, she heard the flapping of what sounded like large wings. Turning her head in all directions, she could see no other birds. *It must be my imagination* she thought flying toward the mountain.

Chapter 7: The People

THE SUN WAS straight up in the sky and Addy was getting hungry. She had flown nonstop since her brief meeting with the owl. Up ahead were rows of strange looking buildings in amongst the trees. Certainly nothing like the forest she had just left. Curiosity took her into the area behind one of the buildings. These surroundings were very different from where she had grown up, for as far as the eye could see each building was surrounded by grass. Not the tall grasses she was used to, but short well maintained grass. There were patches of pretty flowers around the edges of the buildings and grasslands. There were not as many trees, but still enough to accommodate all the birds which were also plentiful. She was surprised how content and happy they all seemed as they went about their day. Addy flew over to a large maple tree. Another robin had the same thought.

"Get out of my tree!" he commanded.

"I am sorry. I didn't know this was your tree," Addy replied. "You live here?"

"I was born and raised in that tree by the brown house over there last spring. Now my mate and I are starting a family of our own," he said, pointing to the nest just above her head. "There is plenty of food and water here. Everything a bird needs to raise a family."

Just then his mate returned shrieking at Addy and almost knocked her off the branch. Without hesitation, Addy flew off, remembering how territorial her breed was. Robins may band together against their enemies, but territories are decided in late winter or early spring and must be recognized as such. She double checked to make sure the next tree she landed in was unoccupied. She thought about the two robins making a family together. It seemed all the robins in this area were paired off. *I wonder if I might be missing something. Enough of that thinking. The sooner I get away from here the better. I do not belong here.* Her thoughts were distracted by another robin down below.

A large concrete pillar stood in a garden of colourful spring flowers. The robin was bathing in it. It was quite unlike any baths she had taken. *No wonder robins have made their homes here. There is plenty of food, water and bathtubs.* She wondered if this was the valley her father had spoken of. Her thoughts were disturbed by the commotion below. Something she had never seen before had come running into the yard towards the bath yelling, "Get away from the bird bath Smokey! Bad cat. Go on now!"

Startled, the robin quickly flew out of the bath into the safety of a distant tree.

My goodness, I didn't even see that cat, Addy thought thinking back to the enemies her father had warned them about. *I have to start being more alert.*

The cat ran away as this creature approached the bath. Another creature had entered into the area with a pail of water and together they refilled the bath. These must be the 'people' her father had warned them about. Addy was confused. *They are our enemies and yet they frightened the cat away and filled the birdbath with more water.*

She thought back to her conversation with Delvin. 'Not all enemies are foes. All creatures, no matter what the species, need to feel connected. Sometimes these connections happen when we least expect them.'

The people walked hand in hand toward Addy.

"Look Mommy. Smokey didn't scare all the robins away," she said pointing up at Addy who remained very still, not sure what to do.

"This one is only a baby," her mother whispered softly. "She still has black spots on her chest."

"How do you know she is a girl robin?"

"Her head is not as black as the males and her breast is a lighter shade of orange."

It felt strange hearing the people describe what she looked like, for she had often wondered.

"She must be on her own. I can't see her parents anywhere," the mother said glancing around the area.

"Is she lost?" the child inquired.

"I don't know," her mother gently replied. "I hope not."

"If I got lost would you come looking for me?"

"Of course I would," her mother answered reassuringly, as she grabbed the girl's tiny hand. "I will always look after you. You can stay with your father and me forever."

"I love you so much Mommy. I am never going to leave you and Daddy."

Addy felt the tears sting her eyes as they walked away. She was more determined than ever to get to the mountain and change the 'law of nature' so she could rejoin her parents. But first some food; she was starving.

Addy flew over into the next patch of grass and began searching for worms. She was finishing off the last of a worm when the loudest squawk she had ever heard pierced the air. Addy froze as she felt the animal's teeth dig into her chest and back. Terror numbed the pain. Her cries for help were drowned out by the animal's pain-filled shriek that opened its mouth releasing her. Stunned and laying on the ground, Addy was not sure if she could fly. She was very dizzy, but faintly aware of the ruckus going on around her.

"Go on! Get out of here! Fly away!" the voice commanded as she tried to regain her senses.

She turned to see a ball of fur and feathers rolling back her way. She staggered a few steps then took flight. She didn't look back and didn't stop flying until the sun was setting behind Magassus Mountain.

Totally exhausted and out of breath Addy landed in the safety of a forest. As she took great gasps of air, she could still feel the animal's teeth penetrating her breast and its hot breath on her body. She wondered if it was the cat the little girl chased away that attacked her. She traced the two tiny lines of dried blood caked on her chest. She parted her feathers revealing two small teeth punctures on her skin.

Though the fresh air had cleared her head, recollection of the horrid incident flooded back. *I could have been killed if it hadn't been for that bird rescuing me...*she stopped in mid-sentence. *Who was that bird?* Her mind flashed back to the scenario. She could see brown markings on white feathers tumbling over and over on the ground with its big yellow feet piercing the animal's back as it screamed in agony. There was something familiar about the bird. But it couldn't be. Any resemblance to Delvin had to be coincidental. He was safe back in the woods they called home. She shuddered as she thought of what had happened to her this morning, yet she would be forever grateful to the mysterious bird that saved her life.

I learned a very valuable lesson today. Mother warned me to never let my guard down and to know where my enemies are at all times. With her mother's voice echoing in her head, she closed her eyes and barely heard the early morning robin's song.

Chapter 8: Edward

EVEN THOUGH HER body ached from yesterday's long flight, her stomach hurt more. She had not eaten since before the animal had attacked her and she was starving. Much more cautious now, she descended to the ground and proceeded to consume anything edible.

As she finished off the last of a June bug, a loud bang sent shivers of panic through her. There was another, then another. She heard a sudden, sharp, explosive noise and watched in horror as the tree she slept in last night split in two and fell nearby. Animals and birds scrambled in every direction as the splintered tree became a burning torch.

"Run for you lives, run for you lives!" echoed through the forest. After another incredibly loud bang, a torrential rainfall ensued coupled with more sonorous bangs paralyzing Addy with fear. She instinctively sank down close to the ground as the rain pelted her back.

"Over here, come over here!" a muffled voice was calling. It was difficult to locate where the voice came from; the intensity of the storm deafened her.

"I am under this log over here. Hurry before the rain washes you away."

Addy ran toward the voice coming from a small space left by a fallen oak tree resting on top of the knoll. The gap was just large enough to accommodate two. To Addy's overwhelming relief, the voice was that of another robin.

"It is not a very nice morning," he said.

"What is happening out there? What are all those loud bangs and flashes of light I sometimes see before the bangs?" she asked anxiously.

"The loud bangs are thunder and the flashes are lightning."

"What does the water falling from the sky mean?"

"That is rain. When you put all the flashing lights, loud bangs, and heavy rains together you get what is known as a thunderstorm. Is this your first encounter with nature's wrath?"

"Yes, and I don't like it," she said with a start, as another clap of thunder shook the ground.

"Scary isn't it? We will have to stay here and wait it out." He looked toward her. "I have never seen you around here before."

She turned her head in his direction. "I am just passing through."

"What is your name? I am Edward."

"Addy."

"It is a pleasure," he said, with a nod of his head.

Addy looked at him and felt her heartbeat quicken. This usually happened when she was frightened. But she was not afraid at all. In fact she felt very relaxed, even as the storm raged on. Edward was very handsome. Even more handsome than J.D. She didn't think any robin could ever measure up to J.D. but Edward certainly did.

Edward ran out into the rain and pulled a large worm out of the soggy ground and brought it back to Addy. Again, as her heart quickened she thanked him.

"So where are you going?" he asked.

"I am on my way to Magassus Mountain," she replied, swallowing a piece of worm.

He knew where the mountain was. "What takes you over to Magassus?" he asked politely.

Addy proceeded to tell him about the crow she had to find. "He knows all about the 'law of nature' and I have got to convince him to change it so I can stay with my parents."

Edward looked at her blankly, for he had never heard of the 'law'. "What is this 'law'?"

"Basically, it is a 'law' stipulating that any offspring cannot stay with their parents if they so choose."

Edward looked perplexed for he had never heard of a robin wanting to stay with its parents forever. Personally, he had not felt that way at all. He shrugged, maybe it happens.

"But aren't you afraid of confronting this crow? Crows are enemies to us."

"I haven't really thought about that part. I just know he is the bird I have to see to get the 'law' changed."

"Addy, it is too dangerous. Maybe you should reconsider. Say, why don't you stay here with me? I will take care of you. Maybe we can be a family."

She tilted her head to one side pondering what Edward had just said. Although what he said felt very comfortable, the urge to return to her parents was far greater.

"Edward, you are very kind and I thank you for your offer, but I must proceed to the mountain and meet with the crow. I know, you can come with me!"

"Oh no, I couldn't do that. It is far too dangerous and besides, I like it here. Next year after migration, I shall choose a mate and bring her back here to start a family."

Addy thought of the paired-off robins in the valley. She felt a small pang of envy for the lucky female Edward would choose.

"For now, why don't you spend a few days here with me? You are not too far from the mountain."

Addy thought of Magassus and sighed deeply. *The rest will do me good.* "I would like that, Edward."

The next few days passed by quicker than either one had anticipated. They enjoyed each other's company, as they were very compatible and became good friends.

That evening as they sat side by side on a branch looking toward the mountain, Addy lost sight of her goal, for she had thoroughly enjoyed her time with Edward. *Maybe it would be okay to stay here with him. But this isn't my home. My home is with my mother and father. Besides, Edward will choose a mate after migration.* Again, she felt that strange twinge of envy. She shook herself and returned to her senses. "I am leaving for Magassus at first light tomorrow."

Edward just stared at the mountain. He was heartbroken for he had hoped she would stay and be his mate for life. "Is there anything I can say or do to make you change your mind?"

"No, Edward. I must do this. I miss my parents so much. I cannot wait to return home and be with them."

Addy fluffed up her feathers bunking down for the night. "Good night, Edward."

"Good night, Addy."

Edward stayed awake the whole night thinking about her. When morning came, they ate together then flew to a tree on the outskirts of the forest.

"I wish you would change your mind, Addy."

"Edward..."

"I know, I know," he interrupted.

"I must go. Good-bye, Edward."

"Good-bye, Addy. It has been nice knowing you..." Edward could hear his voice start to crack and didn't get to finish what he wanted to say. It was too late anyway, she was already gone. As he watched her fly away, he knew he would never love any other robin as he did her. He was so distraught by her departure that he never gave a second thought to a much larger bird that seemed to be in pursuit, yet kept its distance from her.

Chapter 9: Not Goodbye

IT WAS A beautiful sunny day for flying. Not too windy or too hot. There were quite a few clouds in the sky. Big white puffy ones you want to jump into and sleep for a week. Addy had kept up a good pace until hunger pangs signalled it was mealtime. She was over a wide-open area with only a few rocks, shrubs, and tall grasses for shelter. Off into the distance, she could see someone riding on the back of a horse. Luckily, they were riding away from where she was stopping.

She landed close to a small pond which seemed deserted. She was more aware of her surroundings since the animal attack. As she quenched her thirst and glanced around, she felt something wasn't quite right. *I had better eat quickly and be on my way.* She ate some spiders and grass, and then spotted a patch of wild strawberries. She quickly ran over to the tasty morsels and began pulling them from the plants. As she swallowed the last berry, she looked skyward and almost threw it back up. For high above her, the largest bird Addy had ever seen was circling overhead. Judging by its size and the distinctive red tail feathers she knew it was a buzzard hawk.

Don't panic. As long as it remains up there where I can see …It was too late. The hawk was descending too quickly for her to get away. Instinctively, she lowered herself as close to the ground as possible and closed her eyes hoping it would be off target. Suddenly, an ear piercing screech reopened her eyes to see a jumbled mass of feathers rolling over and over less than a metre away.

"Fly away! Get out of here!" the struggling voice commanded. She wasn't sure where the voice was coming from and was not going to stick around to find out. Petrified once again, she took wing. As she flew off, she saw a much smaller bird wrestling with the buzzard hawk.

Again, thankful for her freedom, she flew as quickly as her wings would go. Feeling a little safer, she looked back and to her dismay the hawk was in pursuit. Addy knew she was doomed because the hawk was gaining on her and she could never escape it. The hawk was almost beside her when a thundering boom reverberated throughout the valley sending them both into a tailspin.

"Addy!" the hawk cried out as she tried to gain control of herself. She swung round and watched in horror as the hawk plummeted to the ground. A sick feeling enveloped her, for there was only one hawk that knew her name. She circled back, but dust from the horse's hooves clouded the area as it tore off making it very difficult to see where the hawk had landed.

In a clump of tall grass, the hawk lay sprawled out on its stomach with both wings outstretched from its body. As she got closer, Addy could see its right wing was almost severed. She was unsure if it was still alive. Her approach startled the hawk who raised its head in self-defence.

"Delvin!" she cried. "Oh no! Are you hurt badly? Tell me you will be all right. Please Delvin. It is going to be okay. We will make you better." Addy rambled on hysterically.

"I am alright," he said, as convincingly as possible. The pain was excruciating but he knew he mustn't burden her.

"Why are you here? You are supposed to be home where you would have been safe."

Delvin swallowed hard. "I couldn't bear the thought of you making the journey on your own. I would have worried myself sick. Besides, you would have been too good of a meal for the likes of that cat."

Addy shivered as she thought back to that horrible experience. *So it was the cat the little girl had chased away that had gotten hold of me. And Delvin was the bird that attacked it so I could escape.* "It was you who attacked the cat! You saved my life!" She started to cry. "Now I am going to save yours."

Delvin was moving in and out of consciousness.

"We must do everything we can to get you better. I will stay with you and do all I can."

Delvin's eyes flashed open. "No Addy! You must continue on your journey as you have come such a long way. Another day or two and you will be at the mountain."

Addy looked toward Magassus. What a price the journey had cost. Her best friend had been an easy victim for some hotshot enjoying a little random target practice. Delvin was badly injured.

"There is still some daylight," he said breaking her train of thought. "Please go. You will be there by tomorrow if you leave now."

"No Delvin. I am not leaving you. I will wait until you are better. Then we can finish the journey together."

"It will take me too long to recover and I will only hold you up. You can finish the trek and come back for me. By then I will be my old self once again," he said, as convincingly as possible.

Again, she looked over at the mountain. She could be back for him in a couple of days and then they would return home together.

"Addy, please cover me with lots of tall grass so no one can find me," he said pulling his left wing close to his body. His right wing remained extended as if it no longer belonged to him.

She quickly covered him with lots of grass. "You will be safe from everything now Delvin."

She took note of the location. He had landed beside a small boulder with a large red spot on it. Addy did not realize that it was Delvin's blood that had left the mark when he had fallen onto it before he hit the ground. She also didn't notice the pool of blood he was lying in.

"Good-bye, Addy, and good luck. When your journey is over, go back to Edward. He is waiting for you."

Upon hearing these words, she realized that he had been with her all along.

"No Delvin. I am coming right back here for you and we are going back home together where we belong. I will be back before you know it."

As Addy took off for Magassus, she had no idea that her last words had gone unheard.

Chapter 10: Magassus Mountain

DRIVEN BY HER constant worry about Delvin, Addy flew like she had never flown before. Just before nightfall, she landed in a clump of trees at the base of Magassus Mountain. She was finally here. Mixed emotions enveloped her. Pride and a sense of accomplishment were marred by her worry for Delvin. "Please let him be okay."

She quickly ate then flew to the top of a tall red pine tree. Looking straight up she could not see the top of the mountain. The magnitude of it took her breath away. The mountain slope she observed was heavily wooded.

As darkness descended, she began to wonder how she would locate the crow. Until now, this thought had not occurred to her. Then again, if this crow is as famous as he is made out to be then surely some bird around here must know of his whereabouts.

Though she was very tired, her thoughts were consumed with Delvin. *I will be back to you soon, my friend.* It was the least she could do. He had risked his life for her the moment he left their forest home. The only time woodland hawks leave the woods is during migration. *I will never forgive myself if he doesn't make it. Perish the thought,* she shivered.

It seemed like she had just fallen asleep when a robin's song awoke her instantly at dawn's first light. Stretching her tired wings she thought *I must eat quickly then discover where the crow is located.*

Not far from where she was eating, there were some other robins feeding. She quickly ran over to them.

"Good morning," she said to one of them.

The large male stopped eating.

"Can you please tell me where I can find the cackling crow?"

The three remaining robins stopped feeding and looked at her in disbelief.

"You want to know what?" he asked, unsure he had heard her correctly.

Even though she noted the shocked expressions on all their faces, she proceeded to ask him again. "Do you know where the cackling crow of Magassus Mountain is located?"

"Are you aware of what you are asking?" he said in a tone that made her feel stupid.

She didn't see what the problem was and proceeded to explain why she had to see him, as the other robins moved in closer.

"For starters, he is a crow," one of the other robins chided. "A crow that would make a meal out of you in a minute."

The spots on Addy's breast were a dead giveaway that she was not an adult.

She stood her ground. "I don't care. I will take my chances. I have come too far and overcome too many obstacles to turn back now. I must see the crow. I don't have time to debate this with all of you. Please, if you know of his whereabouts tell me so I can be on my way."

He shook his head and rolled his eyes skyward. "He probably won't even see you. He doesn't communicate with anyone. However, it is your life. Follow me."

She began to wonder about the power this crow seemed to possess. The male robin flew up to one of the taller pines with Addy right behind.

"See that rocky ledge way up there just above that patch of cherry trees," he said pointing upwards. "That is where he resides."

She followed his wing tip taking note of the location. She turned back to the robin. "Thank you for helping me."

"I hope you are not making a big mistake," he replied feeling kind of sorry for her.

"Me too," she said looking up toward the ledge.

"Good luck," he said before quickly flying away.

Addy took a deep breath. "I have got to do this," she said letting go of the pine branch.

Chapter 11: Dempster the Crow

ADDY MADE HER way up the mountain only stopping periodically to get her bearings. The last stop landed her in a large cherry tree overlooking a ledge. From this vantage point, she observed a fairly large area that showed signs of being inhabited, yet there was no one around. *This may be the crow's home.* The area had all the comforts of a home. A portion of the ledge was sheltered by a large grassy overhang. Under the overhang was a messy pile of twigs and sticks. *I wonder if this is his nest,* she contemplated before flying over to the overhang and looking down into it. It was about 60 centimetres across and 25 centimetres high. The inside cup had been intricately woven with soft strips of bark and leaves. Moss and animal fur cushioned the strips for added comfort. Whoever occupied this nest was probably quite large. Tops of cherry trees swayed back and forth at the side of the ledge. The ledge was so sheltered that the wind seemed to blow around it.

She spotted a small pond nearby and checking to make sure no one was around, she landed at the edge, just missing the bones of what might have been a small bird. As she took small sips and glanced around, she couldn't help marvelling at how homey the area was.

"What are you doing on my mountain!" bellowed a voice of authority.

Choking on her last sip of water, she turned quickly to see a large, bedraggled crow confronting her less than a metre away. Her heart started pounding so hard, she was sure it would beat the remaining spots off her breast. She stood frozen and speechless as the crow walked slowly toward her.

"Well, aren't we the nervy one," the crow said, thinking what an easy meal she will make. "I wasn't expecting any company."

Addy now realized why the area was so deserted. The cackling crow of Magassus Mountain was definitely the controlling force. Her whole body matched the size of his head. She knew she could never get away.

"Well, speak up!" he yelled, puffing out his feathers and doubling his size.

"Cat got your tongue? I ate a cat once," he said, seeming to lose his train of thought, but not for long.

Addy took a small step backwards covering her feet in the pond.

"Leaving so soon?" the crow said, stretching his neck to cover the space between them.

She could see her reflection in his large black eyes. She was shaking so hard, tiny ripples started spreading across the pond.

Addy took a deep breath. "Please, I have only come here to ask you to change the 'law of nature'."

The crow reeled backwards flashing a look of shock and disbelief at her.

She quickly realized she had struck a nerve. A very raw nerve, as she continued on. "You do know all about the 'law of nature' don't you?" she asked, questioning his authority.

The crow swallowed hard trying to regain his composure. "Of course I know all about it. Every bird knows the 'law'," he shot back.

Something wasn't right Addy thought as she watched his disheveled chest heaving in and out.

"Well, I think the law should be changed," she persisted.

"That law must never be changed!" he growled gaining back his control.

"Please, I am begging you to change the 'law' so any offspring can remain with its parents if it so desires. I don't want to leave my parents."

The crow stood firm. "All creatures must leave their mother and father to make a life of their own. Your parents gave you life, now it is up to you to live it to the fullest," he replied adamantly.

Addy started to cry. She had travelled all this way for nothing.

The crow watched as the tears rolled down her cheeks triggering something inside he had never experienced before. He felt a lump form in his throat and tears sting his eyes making it difficult for him to speak. He paused and then swallowed hard. "You have to make a life of your own or you will end up old and bitter like me. And the only emotion anyone will feel for you is fear."

Addy took a close look at this big old unkempt crow. "I don't understand," she said wiping away her tears.

"I too didn't want to leave my parents," he confessed. "Nothing turned out the way I wanted it to from day one."

She listened intently as the crow unfolded his life to her.

"There were seven of us youngsters born to very proud, loving parents. There was so much love, why you could have painted the sky with it. I was firstborn, of course. They named me Dempster. I wanted to be named Cornelius after my great grandpappy. He was a big wig down south you know. A real lady's crow. Lived to be 26 years old. Spent the last three years of his life blind as a bat. But he still managed to take care of himself. It would have been such an honor to be named after him. Instead, they stuck me with Dempster. Dempster the crow. No pizzazz there!"

He paused for a moment then carried on. "Things just got worse from then on. I was having a wonderful life.

Parents who loved me. Brothers and sisters to play with. We were one big happy family living harmoniously here on the mountain. Then, one day, my pa and ma said, 'kids, it's time to make a life of your own. You are old enough to take care of yourselves now. It is time to leave the mountain.' Well I wasn't leaving I told them stubbornly. My parents just looked at me and told me 'it is the "law of nature." Every youngster must leave its parents and make a life of its own.' I wanted no part of that, so I remained on the mountain while they all left me. One by one, I watched in disbelief as they flew away to make a life of their own."

Addy cried softly as Dempster recalled this portion of his life.

"Desertion! That's what I call it. I could not believe my parents would desert me. I have never forgiven them," he said bitterly.

Addy felt his words tugging at her heart for she had felt the same.

"So now I live a lonely, solitary life here on the mountain."

Dempster raised his head and looked at Addy. "All I ever wanted was to be loved. I thought that if I stayed with my parents, I would be guaranteed that love."

His deep-seated anger surfaced again. "Instead they left me all alone to fend for myself. I resent them as much now as I did then. I am nothing but a bitter, angry, spiteful, old crow. All I have is this rotten reputation to live up too."

He took a deep breath. "Lonely! Do you have any idea how lonely life up here on the mountain is?"

"Why don't you fly off the mountain and try to find a mate?"

He chuckled softly. "Who would ever have the likes of me? Besides, I am too old and ornery for that stuff," he replied with regret written all over his face.

He looked toward her. "What's your name kid?"

"Addy."

"Well Addy, you are very young and just starting out your life. You have lots of time to get on with it. This is only the beginning of life's adventure for you. Now be wise and brave enough to start living your life to the fullest so you don't end up like me."

"At least you have this beautiful mountain," she said trying to console him.

"This mountain is all I have," he sighed. "I can only dream of how wonderful it would have been if I could have shared it with a mate."

Addy thought of Edward.

"You can talk to the mountain all you want but it won't answer you. I have no offspring to leave it to. I only have the legacy of the cackling crow of Magassus Mountain and it will die with me. At least I have this rotten reputation of being a bad guy," he chuckled, wishing he didn't. "That explains all these lonely years up here, when all I ever wanted was to be loved."

Addy felt sorry for Dempster, but she had learnt a very valuable lesson. She knew she could never live such a lonely life. She gave up all thoughts of returning to her parents. It was time to begin a new life of her own.

Dempster turned toward Addy. "Enough talk about my sorrowful life. All this excitement has made me hungry."

Addy stepped back further into the pond.

Dempster studied the robin. "Oh, relax. I am certainly not going to eat the only guest I have ever had. Who knows? You may want to come back some day and visit again."

Over lunch, they chatted like two old friends. Dempster had many humorous tales about life on the mountain to share. He rambled on and on. Addy figured he had kept all of this bottled up for years. It was such a shame he never shared his life with anyone because he was really an okay crow.

"Dempster, did you know that there is a great horned owl that can make your mountain disappear then reappear?"

Dempster ducked down and looked around at the surrounding trees. "Where is this owl?" he hissed. He knew all too well that one crow, especially one as old as himself was no match for a great horned owl.

She saw the fear on his face and quickly put him at ease. "He is not here Dempster. He is back in some woods where I stayed on my journey to Magassus."

"That's better," he said straightening up. "Now, what about this owl?"

"He made your mountain disappear."

"Oh really. And just how did he manage that?" Dempster asked sarcastically.

"I don't know. This owl claims to be magical. I went to sleep one night and when I awoke the mountain had disappeared. I was in such a hysterical state that the owl told me to go get something to eat and when I was finished, he guaranteed to have the mountain in place. Sure enough, there it was when I returned to my branch."

"Why that sneaky old bird," Dempster growled. "He can't make a mountain disappear then reappear. Nobody can for gosh sakes. You say it was early morning?"

"Yes. Right at dawn's first light."

"It was fog, my dear."

"Fog?"

"Fog. Periodically, the fog gets so thick you cannot see a doggone thing for miles. How dare that owl claim to be so powerful? No one can make my mountain disappear. Not even me."

"I guess there is no sense telling you about the magic trick he can do with his toes," she said, feeling a bit silly for believing the owl's tall tale. She couldn't figure out why

Dempster was so agitated. After all, she was the one who had been fooled.

"Just don't be so gullible," Dempster grumbled. "Especially when it comes to believing a great horned. They will tell you anything."

Addy figured he was upset because he didn't think of it first. "I promise not to be so gullible in the future," she chuckled.

Dempster finished off the last of his lunch then looked at Addy. "Young lady, it is time for you to get going. There is a great big world out there just waiting for you to discover. Don't be a stupid bird like me. The name Dempster means 'one who judges'. I judged wrong and ruined my whole life. Don't you make the same mistake. Now be off with you. I have a reputation to live up to. Cackling crow. Ha! I'll show 'em."

Addy learned a lot about herself today. She was confident enough after all she had been through to make a life of her own now.

"Delvin," she thought aloud.

"Who is Delvin?"

"A dear friend I must go to." Even though she had befriended Dempster, instinctively she knew Delvin's whereabouts must remain a secret. He would be easy prey.

"Delvin; proud friend," Dempster said.

Addy looked at him questioningly.

"That is what the name Delvin means."

"I have got to go," she muttered. "Thank you for everything Dempster. I shall never forget all you have taught me here on Magassus Mountain." Without further ado, she quickly flew off.

He watched as she disappeared from sight wishing it was five years ago when he had had the same opportunity. But for the first time in his life, he felt good about himself.

"At least I saved someone from this same fate," he sighed, as he gazed around the area he called home. "I guess life isn't so bad after all."

"Maybe it isn't too late for me. Father did say `sometimes your first choice might not be the right choice'. I could travel the world telling stories," he chuckled, thinking of the exaggerated tale he told Addy about his great grand pappy.

"She bought that one hook, line and sinker. Yes, I can see it now! Dempster the Crow, a.k.a. story teller and artist. Oh, I almost forgot, star."

Content with himself at last, he walked over to his nest and hopped in. "Nap time."

Chapter 12: Proud Friend

ADDY FLEW AS quickly as she could to Delvin, hoping he had recovered well enough to fly back home. She spotted the boulder with its large red mark and landed on top of it.

"Delvin, it's me, Addy."

There was no answer. She quickly hopped down to the ground and started to pull the grass off him.

"Delvin! Delvin!" *He is probably sleeping* she thought as she continued to pull off his grass cover while talking. "I have some good news. I have met with the cackling crow. His name is Dempster. He is not such a bad crow after all. He helped me to come to terms about leaving my parents. I am not going back to them, Delvin. I am mature and strong enough to make a life of my own now. You should see the size of Dempster," Addy went on as she pulled at the grass. "He is larger than you and me put together," she said, suddenly feeling there was something very wrong.

Addy dropped her beak full of grass and stared at Delvin. He had not moved. In fact, he was in the exact same spot he was when she covered him with grass.

"All he ever wanted was to be loved. Just like you my proud friend," she sputtered through her tears.

Delvin was gone. She had never felt so alone. He had always been close by. She cried and cried until the first light of dawn.

Addy had lost her best friend. Delvin gave his life for her. Nothing mattered any more. She had no one to return home to. She was all alone. Now she knew how Dempster must feel living all alone on the mountain.

She started to re-cover Delvin with grass, and as she did she could hear his last words echoing through her head. "Go back to Edward. He is waiting for you." Addy caught her breath. Even in death, Delvin was still taking care of her.

With tears stinging her eyes, she gently laid down the last sprig of grass.

"I hope you can hear me, Delvin. Oh how I wish you were standing in front of me so I could tell you this face to face."

"Thank you for believing in me and always being there for me, proud friend. I shall never forget you. You will be with me in spirit always."

She turned to leave and whispered, "I love you very much Delvin. Good-bye my dear friend."

Chapter 13: A New Life

WITH ALL THE strength she could muster, Addy flew back to where she had left Edward. She spent the remainder of the day searching the woods for him. As night began to fall she realized her search had been in vain. Edward had moved on.

She had not eaten since her meeting with Dempster and was almost too weary to eat now. She flew down to the ground in search of food. Even pulling a worm was a major undertaking, as the events of the last few days took their toll.

"Here, let me get that for you."

Addy turned in the direction of a familiar voice. "Edward!" she cried running over to him. She was so happy to see him she forgot how exhausted she was.

"Did you complete your journey to Magassus Mountain to get the 'law of nature' changed?" he asked, noting the pained look on her face.

"It is a long story, Edward."

"That's okay. I have got a whole lifetime to hear it. That is if you will give me the honour."

"You mean you still want to share your life with me?"

"Every precious moment."

"Delvin was right. You did wait for me."

"Delvin?"

"My proud friend. A very significant part of the story, Edward."

Edward and Addy finished eating and then flew up into the middle branches of an old birch tree. As they sat side by side, Addy finally felt content for the first time in her life. She now understood the 'law of nature'. Especially now she had Edward to share her life.

This is where I belong, with Edward. She snuggled closer to him.

"Good night, Edward."

"Good night, Addy."

If you enjoyed this book you'll enjoy these:

Jule's Story
by Arlene Johnston,
ISBN: 978-0-9813539-6-8
Published 2010

What would you do if you found out you had a twin from another planet? Read Jule's story to find out what one boy from Haliburton did.

To purchase any of these books as eBooks go to www.pinelakebooks.org
For a complete listing of all titles and genres go to
www.pinelakebooks.ca

Bellus Terra
by Tammy Woodrow,
ISBN: 978-0-9813539-7-5
Published 2010

When they discover their world is in danger, two faylings and a pixie set out to find someone who can save them.

Lorah's Promise
by Ann Harris
ISBN: 978-1-926898-00-1
Published 2010

When her family emigrates from Ireland to the Dominion of Canada in 1868 Lorah faces a multitude of challenges; crossing a raging river in a severe storm, and facing a black bear are only a few. Will she be able to overcome the many challenges she faces and fulfil a promise she has made.

To purchase any of these books as eBooks go to
www.pinelakebooks.org
For a complete listing of all titles and genres go to
www.pinelakebooks.ca

The Ghost in the Dungeon
By Lynn Henderson
ISBN: 978-1-926898-19-3

Sisters Dakota and Rose are staying in a Scottish castle while their father studies whales. When they move in they soon discover their castle is haunted by a young girl, Annabelle, who needs the sisters to help her find her long lost father.